Baby Looking Out and Other Stories

PADMINI MONGIA

Illustrated by
PRIYA KURIYAN

YODA PRESS
79, Gulmohar Enclave
New Delhi 110 049
www.yodapress.co.in

Copyright © Padmini Mongia 2018

Illustrations © Priya Kuriyan 2018

The moral rights of the author have been asserted
Database right YODA PRESS (maker)

All rights reserved. Enquiries concerning reproduction outside the scope of the above should be sent to YODA PRESS at the address above.

ISBN 978-93-82579-23-6

Editors in charge: Sonjuhi Negi, Arpita Das and Apoorva Saini
Typeset by Jojy Philip
Printed at Saurabh Printers Pvt. Ltd.
Published by Arpita Das for YODA PRESS, New Delhi

Contents

Acknowledgements vi

Baby Looking Out 1
The Bat and his Kite 10
The Kachhua and the Daddu 25
Mannoo the Monkey and his Hat 38
The Red Shoe 56
Joey and his Mood 90
Fair and Unfair 106
Soman and the Toot 121
Miss Hadd 143

About the Author 154

Acknowledgements

In remembrance of
Usha Mongia (1932-2017)
Ved Vyas Mongia (1927-1988)

And with thanks to
Naintara and Naira,
the best listeners

Some of these stories are set in Defence Colony in New Delhi and in the house my parents built. This book is dedicated with much love to their memory, as well as to my sisters, nieces, family and friends who share the laughter and joy associated with D 30.

My deepest thanks to Anjana Appachana and Bill Hutson, who not only helped clear the path but also shared the road; to Franklin and Marshall College for helping fund the production of this book; to Julie Daniels, savior-editor; to Priya Kurian for her delightful illustrations; to Arpita Das for taking the chance and Ishita Gupta for her untiring work; and to members of my writing groups in both Lancaster and New Delhi.

Baby Looking Out

Once there was a baby. When his mama held him close to her and cooed in his ear, he fidgeted. Mama held him tighter. He fidgeted again. She put him down. He cried. She picked him up and held him close to her. He fidgeted and tried to turn around. His mother turned him around and held his back to her chest. Then the baby looked happy and moved his head from one side to another. Now he could look out. Now he could see that the waiter was pouring orange juice, Dad was eating too much bacon, and a man was kissing a woman at the next table. At the table after that one, a man was kissing a man. Back at his table, everyone was chatting and eating. Mama was holding him, so she was eating from the side. Dad was looking straight at him as he ate strip after strip of bacon. Grandpa was looking happy, looking at him. A sad woman was looking sad, looking at him. Another man was there, but he was not looking at him. Aunt was at

the other end of the table. She also liked the bacon and was eating strip after strip. Aunt's boyfriend was looking gloomy. He was sitting behind Aunt, as if he wasn't even at the table. Grandma was bubbling with chatter. She kept talking and kept holding Grandpa. That's because Grandpa was very sick. Baby knew that. That's why they'd come, all the way from California to Philadelphia, to see Grandpa. The whole family had come. Grandpa's brother was there, but he wasn't eating breakfast. He had no money to pay for a fancy breakfast in a fancy hotel. But nobody offered him breakfast. So Grandpa's brother picked a piece of bacon from Dad's plate and he picked a muffin from Mama's plate, and then he asked for some coffee, all for himself.

Mama got up and passed the baby to the sad woman. She held him looking out. After a while, she passed the baby to Aunt. Aunt held the baby so he could look out. Then Aunt passed the baby to Grandma. She held the baby, who looked out. Then someone said, "Let's take a family photo." Everyone went downstairs and posed on a sofa. Mama held the baby, looking out. Baby, looking out, stared at the camera like all the other people. The sad lady and the other man took the pictures. They took one picture after another and a light kept going off in everyone's eye. Baby looked down to hide from the light. Mama tried to turn him around, but he fidgeted. Then Mama held him looking out again and he was okay. Then the sad lady said, "This is a baby looking out," and Baby, looking out, looked at her. Everyone agreed he was a baby looking out. They said, "That's a good name for this baby."

Then everyone started saying goodbye. Grandpa and Grandma came and kissed Mama and Baby Looking Out before going back to their room. Grandpa's brother was coming with them, so he did not say goodbye. The sad lady came and stroked Baby's cheek and said goodbye. The man who was not looking at him came and said goodbye. Aunt came and held Baby Looking Out one more time before saying goodbye. Then she gave him a present of a soft green frog and said, "Thank you for coming," to Mama and Papa. Aunt's boyfriend had disappeared. Mama said, "Will you get the baggage?" Dad nodded and said, "Let's meet outside." Mama walked with Baby Looking Out to the window to wait for Dad and Grandpa's brother.

Outside the window, the day was sunny. It was fall, and the leaves were yellow and red and brown on the few small trees in the city. On the street, there were large planters with plants and flowers in them. They were very big. Baby Looking Out saw green leaves with flat sides and pointy ends waving in the breeze. Beneath these leaves were small red ones. Then there were long, thin stalks in a darker green. Some leaves were red with black stripes inside. Their edges were curly. Baby Looking Out liked the planters. Then Baby Looking Out turned his head to the right and saw that there was one planter after another all the way down the street to City Hall. In every planter, plants were waving. In the next planter, on top of the waving plants, a man was sleeping. He was curled up; his knees were pulled up to his chest, and his head lay on his hands. People were walking past him as if he was a plant. The man looked old and dirty, but he was sleeping and sleeping. Then Baby Looking Out looked to the left. There were planters and planters all the way down the road. There were no men sleeping in these planters. Then Mama said, "Let's go stand outside and see if Dad is

coming." She walked to the front of the hotel to the many glass doors, and then she pushed one. Now they were on the street.

Outside the hotel was a man in a black coat and black pants and a black hat. His coat had lines of gold running around the sleeves. His pants had lines of gold running down the sides. His hat had a broad line of gold around it. The man was helping people put bags in their cars. He smiled at the people, lifted bags off the trolley another man brought from inside the hotel, and then he held their car doors open. When the people got in their cars and shut their car doors, they handed the man something crumpled. The man in the black coat said thank you and bowed his head. The people getting in the cars also nodded their heads slightly. Then they drove away, and the man in the black pants and black coat with the gold stripes put the crumpled thing into his pocket. Then he did everything all over again.

Mama cooed at her baby. She shifted him from one side of her body to the other, but she still held him looking out. She leaned around him and gave him a nice kiss on the side. The sad lady came with the man who was not looking at the baby. The sad lady said, "Oh, here you are still," and Mama said, "Yes, we are waiting for Dad and the car." The sad lady nodded. Then she cooed at the baby and said, "Here's Baby Looking Out." She was quiet for a minute and then she said, "I wonder what he sees." She was looking straight at the baby. Baby Looking Out was looking straight at her. The man with the sad lady said, "I think the baby sees you." Everybody laughed. Then the sad lady and the man said bye again and walked away. Mama said, "What do you see, Baby, what do you see?" She was looking at him from around the side. She wanted the baby to answer, but he didn't. She said, "Baby, my mother always said, 'No matter what you see, there is much more that you don't see.' Do you hear that, Baby? Whatever you're looking at, look again; there's more you'll see. Can you understand that?" Baby Looking Out heard that and tried to see again. He saw the same things he had seen. He saw so many things. Didn't he see all there was to see?

Baby Looking Out looked and looked again. He looked at the planter. He saw that in the planter there was a crumpled brown paper bag beneath the red leaves. Baby Looking Out was surprised. Was the bag there before? If it was, why hadn't he seen it? Baby didn't like that. Then he looked again at the next planter where the man was still sleeping. Then Baby Looking Out saw that the man was brown, like the paper bag, only darker. Baby had not noticed that before.

He looked back to the man helping people with their bags. He was also dark brown. Then Baby looked at his mother's hand. It was also dark, but it was a lighter dark. Baby's own hand was even lighter than Mama's hand. All the people coming out of the hotel were pink and white. All the people helping them were dark and brown. The man who pushed the trolley with the bags was as dark as the man helping to put the bags in the car. They were the same colour as the man who was a plant. The people who drove away in their cars were pink and white.

Many people came down the street. Most of them were pink and white. They were walking in ones and twos and threes. The twos were holding hands. The ones looked as if they were rushing somewhere important. The threes were just strolling along. Many ones had fat newspapers under their arms. Many ones and twos and threes were talking on small phones as they walked along. Then Dad's voice said, "Here we are." Dad had brought the car, and Grandpa's brother was with the bags. The dark man in the black coat and the black pants helped Grandpa's brother with the bags. Baby saw that Grandpa's brother was a very dark black. He was short and fat and wore glasses. His whiskers were long and full. Grandpa's brother always touched his whiskers. Dad did not have whiskers. He was very light, lighter than all the others. Dad was a big man who didn't speak very much. His tummy was large and round. Baby Looking Out liked to sit on that tummy. Sometimes Dad would put him on his tummy and fall asleep. Baby liked that.

All the bags were now in the car. Mama put Baby in a seat in the back and strapped him in. Then she got in next to him. Dad handed something crumpled to the man holding the car door. Grandpa's brother sat next to Dad in front. Then Dad said, "Ready?" and Mama said, "Ready." Then Dad started the car and drove up the street towards City Hall. Baby Looking Out could not see that. He was facing the back of the car. If he looked straight ahead, he could only see the back of the back seat. If he looked up a little, he could see a window and some light. He could see blue sky and no clouds outside. Sometimes a tree would pass by. If Baby looked to the side, he could only see the car door. If he looked to the side and up, he could see the car window. Through the car window, he could see the sky and he could see parts of buildings pass by. Sometimes a tree would pass by in front of the building. If Baby looked to the other side, he could see his mother. She was looking at him. She was looking happy. His mother was large and round and cheerful. She said, "That was a nice visit, wasn't it?" Dad said, "Yes, it was." Grandpa's brother nodded yes. Then Mama said, "Your dad is a very good painter. And he has such interesting friends." Dad didn't answer, but he nodded. Mama said, "Why does Alice's boyfriend never speak? Where did he disappear?" Baby knew Mama was talking about Aunt and her boyfriend. Dad didn't answer. He just made a funny sound from inside his belly. Grandpa's brother said, "Well, I suppose he doesn't like to speak. Maybe that's why he disappeared." Mama nodded, but she still looked puzzled.

They rode in silence for a while. Then Dad said, "We're almost there. Is Baby okay?" Mama nodded and said, "Baby's looking sleepy. Well, he's behaved very well, no? He should have a nap." She looked for Baby's bottle and put a nipple in his mouth. Baby Looking Out was not sleepy, but he was tired of looking. He had seen twice. He thought if he saw the same things again, he would see more things. But he felt tired. So he sucked on his bottle and started closing his eyes. Soon Baby Looking Out was fast asleep. He slept through the airport and through most of the flight. Even when he woke up, he didn't look out. Instead, he stayed on his father's tummy, with his head against his chest, and he just stared, looking at nothing.

The Bat and his Kite

Once there was a blackish and brownish and greyish and yellowish bat. His ears were pointy and his eyes were sharp and bright. His fingers and claws were nice and strong, and he liked to show off their strength by hanging upside down for hours without moving. All the other boy and girl bats were jealous of how strong Pond was, and Pond loved to see their watchful eyes peeping at him when all the bat children practised hanging upside down. And yes, he was called Pond, even though Pond wasn't the name he was given by his mother when he was born. No, she had called him Chipku, because she wanted him to *chipko* to roofs and hang upside down for long hours. He did, but he also chipkoed to her all the time. She would tease Chipku and say, "You should have been a kangaroo; you never leave your mother alone." But Chipku was not the name he became known by. Instead, soon after Chipku grew a little, everyone started calling him Pond, because he had almost fallen into one well before his first birthday.

In the house where Pond lived with his family and his mother's and father's brothers and sisters and their husbands and wives and their brothers and sisters and their families—eighty-eight bats in all, more or less—there was actually a pond. The family who lived in this house was very proud of the pond. In the evenings, they came outside with their tall, icy drinks and stood around the pond to talk about the little lotus flowers trying to grow. The father said, "When the lotus flowers are bigger, we can have a party around the pond," and the mother nodded as she gazed at the flowers. The party never happened because soon everyone realised that the pond was also much loved by the many mosquitoes that lived nearby. There were so many mosquitoes that the pond had to be closed over with mud before many years had passed, much to the regret of the bats who loved the easy snack of mosquitoes. By then, Pond, still quite small, had almost fallen in when he had just started practising strengthening his claws and fingers for hanging.

Here's how it happened. Inside the house where the bats lived was a beautiful, handsome staircase. The stairs were wide and the banisters were of smooth, dark teak wood that had come all the way from Burma. The wood curved along the stairs and tempted hands to slide its entire length, whether the hands were going up or going down. The stairs were hardly used and rarely cleaned. They led up to a large terrace, but nobody used it except the cook who climbed it using the back stairs. At the top of the first landing of the handsome staircase, just where the stairs curved, the ceiling was very, very high. Almost where the ceiling ended was a funny window that was more a skylight than a window. But there was no glass in the space that was the skylight. Instead,

there was an intricate pattern made of concrete that decorated the skylight space in the wall. Through this space the light came in and the air came in and sometimes a bird stumbled in. It was the favourite space of all the bats. Even though they lived (all eighty-eight of them, more or less) in and around the staircase and behind the paintings and baskets and hats that hung along the walls, the skylight that was part open and part closed was the perfect space where everyone wanted to sleep. Here bats would take turns to hang upside down and snooze in the fresh breeze blowing in from outside where the garden and the pond were. But everybody could not fit in this space, so the bats had to take turns sleeping there.

One day, when Pond was just a baby, he was taken to the skylight by his mother, who herself had grown up in a cave in the mountains and knew that bats slept better if they breathed fresh air. Pond was still new to hanging, but he was not new to showing off. When he and his mother flew to the latticed concrete of the skylight that was and was not one, his mother said, "Chipku, be careful. Don't be showing…," but

she never finished her sentence. Pond was on his way down and out. He had fallen out of the trellised concrete, and his mother followed right behind and not a minute too soon because she saved him just as he was about to land on the watery pond! She quickly flew him back inside the stairwell and regretfully gave up her favourite place for sleeping to another bat. She scolded Pond strongly. "Chipku," she said, "look what you did. You have to learn not to show off. You were about to fall right into that pond because you wanted to show everybody that you can chipko better than all the others. It's lucky that I saw you and flew out right away or you'd be in trouble. You're not one of the bats that can go fishing in water." Pond was shivering in fear. He had been planning to hang without twitching so he could impress his friends Ranu and Thothla. Instead, he had seen the grey pond with its bright lotus flowers zooming up to meet him as he fell.

Even though he hadn't actually landed on the water, the story of Chipku's (almost) fall into the pond was told and re-told by all the mothers to their children so they wouldn't show off while they practised hanging upside down. "Remember

how Chipku didn't chipko and almost fell into the pond? That's what will happen to you if you start showing off. You're a bat. You're supposed to hang. But you can twitch, too. You don't have to hang without twitching for hours and hours," the mothers would repeatedly warn their children. The bat children would nod their understanding, but they kept trying to hang without twitching anyway. Pond was the one who could hang for the longest, and maybe that's why the children stopped calling him Chipku and started calling him Pond instead. It was a way to tease him and remind him that even though he was strong and could hang for hours without twitching, he was a bat who had (almost) fallen into a pond.

At first, Pond was embarrassed by his new name. Then he wasn't, because Pond was so strong that he could hang for longer than any of the bats in his large family of eighty-eight bats (more or less) who lived in the stairwell. Besides, Pond knew that all the other bat children wanted to be him, and it wasn't because he could hang so well. No, it was because Pond had a pink kite that he would fly at night when the moon was round. What all the other bat children wanted was a kite like Pond's and the skill to fly it zigzagging against the white light of the full moon.

Pond had found the kite many months ago. Because he was learning to hang without twitching and was already trying to show off, he had started practising hanging whenever he could. It didn't matter if it was day or night. After he had eaten enough nectar, Pond would hang and hang and hang. He got bored hanging, so he always tried to choose new places to practise. Sometimes he hung behind a basket in the stairwell. Sometimes he hung under the leaves of the banyan tree. Sometimes he hung under the small balconies of the house. One day, he decided to hang on the jamun tree that grew in the corner of the garden. The tree was tall and had thick, dark leaves. It was a good place to practise, because nobody could see him hidden in the leaves. Pond liked to be alone, even though it was hard for him to be alone, since he was so popular. The other bat children always followed him thinking he was having more fun than they were. But Pond was clever. He knew how to hide from others. "I have to go on a special errand for my mother," he said to the bat children flying around him. "It's an internal family errand and a secret." The bat children were impressed. First, Pond was being sent on an errand, which was rare. Most bats did their running around themselves. Then the errand was an internal family secret. Although the children didn't know what this meant and neither did Pond, it sounded so impressive that they quietly scattered away and went to play different games. Pond looked around him carefully, flew first to the pond and visited the small lotus flowers there, and then flew to the opposite side of the garden where the straggly peach tree grew. Only after he had hidden in the peach for some time did he quietly fly behind it and find his way to the thick leaves of the jamun. There, on a high branch, Pond perched upside down.

First he did a few pull-ups. Then he breathed deeply. Then he looked from left to right, and seeing that all was quiet, he allowed himself to relax into his hang. Time passed. Pond didn't twitch, but he allowed the breeze in the tree to rock him gently. Every so often he would open his eyes and let them look around. From the corner of his eyes, he could see the lotus flowers on the pond. They were just drops of pink, but they were unmistakable. If Pond let his eyes move to the right, he could see the white front gate of the house where he lived. If he looked above him, he saw a canopy of green. If he looked below, he saw the brown earth. Pond was wonderfully relaxed. The light was going down slowly as he hung and hung and hung. It was time for his eyes to do another tour of the garden. Once again, Pond let his eyes move from one side to another. Once again he saw the pink lotus flowers, the green canopy above, the white gate on the right, and the brown earth below. Pond began enjoying this round of colour and let his eyes circle around the pink, green, white and brown while his body stayed completely still and strong. Round and round he let his eyes travel, making the colours whirl faster and faster—pink, green, white, brown, pinkgreenwhitebrown, pinkgreenwhitebrown—when suddenly, the perfect whirl was disturbed. Pinkgreenwhitebrown became pinkgreenpinkwhite and Pond never got to the brown because his eyes went straight back to the greenpink.

Puzzled by the greenpink, Pond stopped his circle of colour. How had the pink of the lotus flowers in the pond landed in the green canopy above him? Pond shut his eyes and thought carefully. Had he changed direction? Had he just confused himself by whirling around the colours too fast? That must be it, he thought. He must have become dizzy with the whirling colours because he had been rushing through them. It was like the game of *keekalikalee* that he played with the bat children, when they held each other's hands and whirled round and round until they fell down in a heap, laughing, giggling and dizzy with everything circling in a blur around them. That's right. That must've been what happened to his whirling eyes even though his body was perfectly still. His eyes had been playing keekalikalee and had become dizzy, and blurred all the colours together. So Pond shut his eyes and kept them pressed tightly. Everything was nice and dark and soft black inside his eyes. For some moments, Pond enjoyed the soothing warmth of the soft black. There was no pink under his eyes, and no green, and no white. Just soft black. Then slowly Pond opened his eyes. He did not look up. No. First he looked at the pond again. He was glad to see the drops of pink there. Then he looked to the right. He saw the clear white of the gate. Below him, the brown earth was brown. Then taking a deep breath, Pond let his gaze travel to the green cover over his head. The dark green leaves of the jamun made everything slightly green around him, so Pond's eyes travelled slowly along the green glow until they reached the green cover over his head. There, amidst the thick jamun leaves, was an unmistakeable touch of pink.

Pond gazed at the greenpink. What was the pink doing with the green? He knew he should fly to the top of the tree and find out. But Pond was in a bind. He was enjoying one of the longest and most soothing hangs he had ever had in his life. He was not tired. He was not bored. Even though he had been hanging for hours, the green was so delicious, so soft, so enclosing, that he didn't want to move. Besides, Pond was competing with himself. He already knew he had never

hung for so long without moving before. He wanted to hang even longer. But his gaze kept travelling to the pink above his head, as he puzzled over what was there. He couldn't tell. The pink was the same pink as the lotus on the pond. But it was impossible for the lotus to have landed on the treetop. So, what was that pink? Now, try though he did, Pond's concentration was gone. No longer were his eyes pleased to circle their round of colour. His body started twitching even though he tried to stay still. And then in a jiffy Pond suddenly broke his hang and flew up to find out how the pink from the pond got into the green above his head.

Of course there was no lotus flower growing in the jamun leaves. Instead, what Pond found was a small kite, a kite made of thin kite-paper, with a long thread trailing beneath it for flying the kite. Even though the kite had landed in the leaves, there was no tear in it. Pond had seen many kites before. They were always gnarled in trees, and the young bat children loved to play in them and tear their thin paper off. They played games to guess what the rustle of the kite-paper sounded like, and then they fought amongst themselves to get portions of their bamboo frames to chew on. But the kite Pond had found was not like any he had ever seen. This one was tiny, a perfect, small kite, just the right size for a bat to fly.

Pond gently moved the kite this way and that to get it away from the leaves. Then he gazed at it and marvelled at how perfect it was. Its bamboo frame was strong and taut, held together with a matching pink thread. The string to fly the kite was also pink. Pond wanted to fly the kite, but he did not know how. He had seen many children fly kites. All over the city, children rushed out to rooftops to fly kites, especially on the windy days just before the monsoon. Pond had seen the children pull the thread, zigzagging it until the kite soared high into the sky. That's what he wanted to do, but he wondered how. He had no idea. Then Pond decided to try to fly with the kite. Pond had never flown with a kite before, but he was sure he could do it. Well, he wasn't sure, really. He knew he had to try to do so to be absolutely certain that he could. So he did a little experimental flight holding the string of the kite in his mouth. It was easy. The kite was the perfect size for him. As Pond flew over the jamun tree and towards the straggly peach, he slowly moved further down the string, so the kite started soaring behind him. Soon Pond was holding the kite by the very end of the string, and behind him a flash of pink followed bobbing in the air.

After circling the garden a few times, Pond decided to return home with his find. When he entered the stairwell through the skylight that was and was not one, all the other bats were busily going about their business. They stopped and stared at the sudden pink that had entered their home. Pond stood on a basket that was hanging high on the side of the staircase and held his kite aloft. He didn't speak at first, while he enjoyed everyone (almost all eighty-eight bats, more or less) staring at him in wonder. "Where did you get that?" asked Ranu at the same moment as Pond's mother said, "Where have you been? I've been so worried! And where on earth did you find that? Is it a kite?" Pond nodded yes, looking very pleased. "Yes, I've found a kite," he said. "I've found a kite that's the right size for a bat. Please come outside and see me with it." With that, Pond flew out to the terrace, and all eighty-eight bats (more or less) eagerly followed him.

Night had just fallen, and the moon was casting its white glow over the jamun tree, the straggly peach tree, and the pink lotuses in the pond. The white gate looked even whiter and brighter in the light of the moon. Pond wished he could stand on the terrace and fly the kite as he had seen children do, but he couldn't. He knew he would have to learn to fly a kite to be able to do that. But he could fly with a kite, and that was also fun. So he said, "I don't know how to fly the kite yet, but I hope I will soon. Now I'll show you how I can fly with the kite." Then he put the end of the long string of the kite in his mouth and soared away as far as he could go. He knew the moon was behind him and he knew he must be looking striking with his blackish and brownish and greyish and yellowish hair trailing a bright pink kite behind him. Farther and farther he went, and all the eighty-eight bats (more or less) of his family were thrilled to see him look so handsome outlined against the moon. The bat children whispered to each other in envy, and they started wailing, "I also want a pink kite to fly, I also want a pink kite to fly," and the mothers patted their heads to soothe them and said, "You'll have to get lucky like Pond did and find a kite somewhere." Then Pond swerved around in the sky and came back proudly with his kite. As soon as he landed, he handed the kite to Ranu and Thothla, and said, "Here, why don't you fly with the kite?" And Ranu and Thothla beamed in delight, and both asked hesitantly, "But can I do it?" and Pond said, "Of course you can. You saw how I did it." Then Pond showed them what to do, and first Ranu did what Pond said, and then Thothla flew with the kite while all the other bats gazed in wonder and excitement.

Many bat children flew with the kite that night and on many other nights. The kite was given a special place on the wall in the stairwell. It was carefully tucked behind a basket, and nobody came and slept there for the fear of tearing the kite. Every bat knew that the kite was a very, very rare find and that they had to look after it. So they did. Even though Pond was generous with his kite, all the bat children secretly wanted it themselves. Sometimes they would whisper that to their mothers when they were being put to bed. The mothers would scold their children and say, "You're so lucky that you're a bat who can fly a kite. How many bats do you think there are in this world who can fly kites? And Pond is so generous with his kite, it might as well be yours."

Then the children would nod with slightly shamefaced looks and go to sleep.

Pond was very generous with his kite, but nobody ever used it without first asking him if they could. Pond usually said yes, unless he was planning to fly it himself. He had not been happy just to fly with the kite. No. The very next evening after he found his kite, he had gone flying over the rooftops of the city to watch how children flew kites. He saw them run with the kite to get wind into it before the kite started soaring. Then he noticed how they pulled the string to keep the kite in the sky, flying higher and higher, but in a steady zigzag. Pond quickly saw that it wasn't hard to fly a kite, especially for bats. He didn't have to run with the kite to start it soaring in the sky. No. He could take off from his terrace, get a good flight going, and then start skimming back down while letting the kite trail high in the sky behind him. Pond did, and soon he was flying the kite as if he had always known how.

Pond never fell from a hang after the time when he had almost fallen into the pond. Soon the pond was gone, covered over with mud. Different bamboos and a tiger palm grew where the pink lotus flowers used to be. The eighty-eight bats (more or less) were sorry to lose their snack of mosquitoes, and Pond was sad to see the flowers go. But whenever Pond flew his kite and saw it against the white light of the moon, he thought of the lotus flowers and knew he was lucky to be a bat with a kite to fly.

The Kachhua and the Daddu

The *kachhua*'s house had received quite a battering. Large rain drops and a few hailstones had fallen through the night. Sometimes the kachhua liked to have the rain and hail on his house. If the hailstones were large ones, he liked to play a game dodging them. It was not easy, since he moved slowly, and  gracefully, and thoughtfully. Even though he almost always lost his game and the hail landed on him from all sides, he still found the game fun. Large raindrops on his house were less fun. Sometimes they came and plopped on his back, and the kachhua was not so happy with all the wetness on and below him. During those times, he often put his head right back into his nice, hard shell, and went and hid under a stone or beneath the large, sheltering leaf of the *arbi* plant.

The kachhua lived near a pond in a house in Delhi. He was also called Kachhua because he was the only kachhua who lived there. He and the arbi were good friends. The large leaves of the arbi sheltered Kachhua in the rain and in the heat. Arbi liked Kachhua because he always told lovely stories

of his travels. Even though he moved very slowly, he had lived a long time and had had many travels. He was also a wonderful and funny storyteller. Often, on lazy sunny afternoons, he sat under the arbi, moved his head around from side to side, and told stories of when he had crossed the street or when he had journeyed to the trash dumps near the market.

The morning after the storm in which hailstones and raindrops had fallen on Kachhua, he awoke fresh and clean. Not a sign of the storm from the night before could be seen. The sky was a bright blue. All the leaves were shining after the rain-polish they had received. The dust on the ground had settled nice and flat so that even the mud was a shiny brown. The pond was full of water, and the little lotus flowers in the pond had opened bright and pink to the bright sun. The arbi, on the edge of the pond, was looking particularly striking. Its large, broad leaves were glossy after the rain, and it puffed itself up even more to show off how handsome and strong it looked. Kachhua was enjoying this relaxed morning. "Quite a storm that was, wasn't it?" he said conversationally to Arbi who shook his leaves in agreement. Even Lulu, the lotus, who was usually very shy, piped up in a small voice, "I thought I would break in the rain. And those hailstones were so hard on my nose."

Kachhua and Arbi looked at the delicate lotus and nodded in sympathy. At least Kachhua had a hard shell to protect him and Arbi was a strong plant with big, thick leaves. Yes, the storm must have been worse for Lulu. Neither the kachhua nor the arbi had thought much about how the storm affected the lotus. Now they did. Arbi said, "You know, I wonder how the spider plant was in the storm? It's even smaller than you are, Lulu." The kachhua, the arbi, and the lotus all looked in the direction of the spider plant. It was looking very sad. "I thought you'd never ask," he said. "I lost so many leaves last night." True enough, all around the spider plant lay the broken green leaves of the plant. While the rest of the plants in the pond commiserated with the spider plant, he busied himself with trying to look less miserable than he was feeling. "I feel raw," he said, "and the sun hurts," and he tried to turn the edges of his arms inwards so the sun wouldn't shine so strongly on his fresh wounds. "I wish I was like you, Kachhua," he said, "I wish I had my house with me so that I could crawl into it any time I wanted."

Kachhua nodded in sympathy. He did think he was one of the luckiest creatures because he carried his house with him. "Yes, I am a lucky fellow," he said and pulled his head up higher so everyone could be a little bit jealous of him. "Nobody else carries his house with him," he said proudly. "I was made to travel, I guess. You know, one time...," and everyone knew that Kachhua was beginning one of his stories of some journey he had taken. "Tell, tell," said Arbi, when there was a rude sound. It was Padu the *daddu*, the large toad that lived on the other side of the pond. "*You* were made to travel?" he said, in his deep, crackly voice. "You can hardly move with that big, brown house on your

back. *I* was made to travel," and saying that he exhibited some very spectacular jumps with a few splendid flourishes. One second he was here and the next he was there, near the straggly peach. Nobody had even seen him move, he moved so fast, but he croaked in his crackly voice from there and said, "Let's talk about travel. You, Kachhua, have crossed the street. I, my dear, have seen the world," and with that he was back under the arbi plant, ready to begin one of his stories. "I am perfect for travel," he continued, "with my speed, my grace, and my body made for adventures." Then he sucked in and out and let everyone see how his throat moved as he sucked in the air. The green specks on him and the white specks on him were all shining, after their bath in the rain. Padu looked impressive, but nobody really wanted to hear his story.

"Uff," said Lulu. "Let Kachhua speak, no? Because he travels with his house, it's more interesting, isn't it?" Padu did not agree. "Has he been to Old Delhi? I have," and he puffed out his chest proudly. "Kachhua has only been to the dumpster," said Padu scornfully, when Kachhua spoke: "Padu, stop showing off. Fine, you can move fast, but I have lived and lived and lived. I have stories to tell that you can't even dream of. Did I tell you of the time I travelled on my roller blades? I mean, roller blade!" Kachhua stopped talking. In the surprised silence that fell around him, he drew out a pipe and started getting it ready for a leisurely smoke. Everyone was quiet, even Padu. Eventually, in a small voice, Padu asked, "What are roller blades, Kachhua?" and Kachhua looked proudly from Padu to Arbi to Lulu and said, "I'll tell the story. Let me just get my pipe going."

For Kachhua to get his pipe going was not easy. He had to get the matches out from under the stones at the edge of the garden. Everyone knew they were kept there. "Padu, could you get me my matches, so I may start my story?" he asked, and Padu jumped across in a flash, so keen was he to hear the tale. What were roller blades, wondered Padu, as he waited eagerly with everyone else to hear Kachhua's story. Kachhua was enjoying the attention. Everyone was looking most eagerly at him, as he puffed on his pipe. "Roller blades are these things that have wheels on them. You stand on the platform on the wheels and you can go and go and go. Children like them. Haven't you seen them in the park, Padu, on their roller blades?" Padu had. "Oooooh," he said, understanding what roller blades were. "But how did you get roller blades? Don't they have to fit you? How could you get roller blades?"

"Well," said Kachhua, "that's the story. That, my dear, I mean, my dears, *is* the story. Indeed, how did I get roller blades? I mean, how did I get a roller blade? Well, it happened a long time ago. It was in the park on the other side of these houses. You know, it was a strange day. I had woken up that morning feeling funny. The sun never came out that morning. It was not cloudy, either. It was just a day that refused to wake up. Everything was grey and heavy. It was as if the sun and the day had decided that they were going to sleep and sleep and sleep. All day. Everyone was in a bad mood. Your grandfather, Arbi, folded his leaves and glared at everyone from behind the folds. You, Lulu, you were not born yet. You had yet to be brought from the nursery. And you, Padu, your grandfather got so jumpy that day that he's the one who suggested we go to the park. Yes, he came up to me and said, 'This is a terrible day. It's a day that refused to get up. That happens sometimes. But it's a terrible thing for everyone. You don't know how to get through the day, so let's go for a stroll to the park.' Your grandfather, Padu, was not a slow walker. Like you, he liked to show off. But on that day, he decided to walk slowly along with me all the way to the park. It took us a long time. You know how I am. Sometimes your grandfather, Daddu, would jump ahead and then come back, just so he wouldn't get too restless walking slowly.

"When we got to the park, everything was quiet. No children were playing on the swings. No children were crawling in and out of the monkey bars. No old people were walking up and down. It was quiet and grey and sad, just like the day was. We walked over to the pond in the middle of the park. The lotus flowers there had folded up and were sitting all tight and closed. We sat on the edge of the pond and looked around us sadly, wondering how the time would pass. On the other side of the pond, we could see the pathway that had just been paved. Neither of us had anything much to say. So we were quiet and just staring. The trees were quiet, the flowers were quiet, even the wind was still and silent. I think we were both falling asleep when something funny happened. On the edge of the pond, on the side away from where we were sitting, we suddenly saw a tall, pointy, green thing floating along. All we could see was this pointy, green thing. It skimmed along behind the edge of the pond. We both saw it at the same time. 'Hey,' I said, 'What's that?' Just as your grandfather, Daddu, said, 'Hey, what's that?' We both looked at each other in amazement. The green, pointy thing moved along the edge of the pond and behind it. Back and forth, it was gliding along. It was shiny and it had a bell on the top of its point.

"After we had both stared for a while, I said, 'I think it's a hat.' 'Don't be silly,' said your grandfather. 'How can it be a hat?' 'Because it looks like one,' I answered and started walking towards it. We both walked very, very silently. We walked along the rim of the pond, and soon we were on the other side. I think your grandfather, Daddu, was scared. He didn't even dash ahead as he normally did. When we got to the other side, we had a big surprise. There, beneath us, below the edge of the pond, was a tiny man with a pointy green hat. His clothes were also green, but they had large pink dots on them. The green was shiny and so was the pink. His clothes ended in funny points. There was a pointy edge to his tunic. There was a pointy edge to his pants. But the strangest thing was what he was wearing on his feet. His shoes were pointy, very, very pointy. They were also green and pink. But beneath his feet, that's where the surprise was. Beneath his feet were black platforms. And beneath the platforms, were small wheels. The pointy green man was whizzing along on these wheels. That's why we'd seen him skimming along. From where we had been sitting, we had only seen the top of his head. We had only seen his hat floating along as the man skimmed along on his roller blades.

"Of course, we didn't know they were roller blades. We had never seen anything that looked like this before. Your grandfather spoke first. 'Hey,' he said, and his croaky, crackling voice surprised the man below us. The green man stopped suddenly and looked up at us suspiciously. 'Excuse me?' he asked, and your grandfather,

Daddu, said in a slightly more friendly voice, 'Hey, how are you?' 'Very well,' answered the green man politely. 'How are you?' 'Well, well,' answered your grandfather, and I nodded my greeting as well. 'So,' said your grandfather, 'What are you doing?' 'Roller blading, of course,' answered the green man and started skimming along again. Now he was showing off. First he whizzed back and forth once or twice. Then suddenly he made a circle and then another and then another until we were dizzy watching him. And then, he put one foot up and behind him and made another circle before settling down into skimming once again. Then he stopped and looked at us. 'It's fun,' he said, 'especially on such a grey day. Don't you all have sun here?' I was offended. 'Of course, we have sun,' I answered. 'We have sun every day. It's just that today the sun didn't want to get up and the day didn't want to get up. It's not every day that it happens.' The green man nodded and started skating again. 'Well,' he said, 'I'm glad I'm not from here. Where I come from, the sun wakes up every day.' 'Where do you come from?' asked Daddu, and the little man answered, 'BlatisStock.' 'Where's that?' asked your grandfather, and the green man answered, 'Near Kohana.' We had never heard of these places, but we didn't want the green man to know. So we both nodded yes, and said, 'Oh.' Then we sat quietly and watched the green man skim and twirl and skim and twirl.

"After a while, it was too much to keep watching the green man enjoy himself and show off. I started gliding in and out of my shell. The green man stopped and said, 'Wow, that's nice. Where do you go when you go in there?' 'Home,' I answered carelessly. 'I go home. I carry my home with me. I'm a lucky one.' Then your grandfather said, 'And I'm a lucky one because I can hop and hop and hop and get places in a jiffy. And I don't need roller blades.' And then Daddu, your grandfather, jumped off the edge of the pond and back on the edge and onto a folded sleeping lotus leaf and back to the edge until all we could see was a streak of green and white against the grey day. 'Luckkky,' said the green man, looking impressed. 'But I'm a magician. I can have roller blades if I want or wings if I want,' and in a second the roller blades were sitting empty on the path, and the green man was whizzing around us like a dragon fly. Then he stopped, went back down, and stared at the roller blades. 'Do you want these?' he asked. 'I'm sick of them. I think I'm going to fly away now.' 'Wait, wait,' I said, 'I want the roller blades. But they won't fit me. Can you make them fit me? Then I can go as fast as Daddu.' 'Sure,' said the green man obligingly. 'Come on down first so I can size you.' I slowly crawled down, and he took a good look at me. He tapped my shell, just out of curiosity, and then said, 'I'll have to try that sometime. Carry my house on my back. That will be a treat. I like that.' Then he smiled widely and blew on the roller blades lying on the ground. Before you knew it, they were different. Now there was only one and it was round and it was just my size! But how was I supposed to climb on to that roller blade? I stared at them and then looked at the green man, wondering what to do. The green man saw my problem. 'Design flaw,' he said, and then he blew on the roller blade again. Now there was a long thing that stretched out behind the roller blade. I crawled up onto it and got on to the roller blade. 'Retractable,' said the green man, and pressed a button. The long slide magically disappeared inside the roller blade. 'See how it works,' he said, as I nodded. 'Now off you go.'

"It was not so easy. How was I to go? I couldn't move at all. 'Oops,' he said. 'Another design flaw,' and then he blew again. This time, he pointed out another button. 'Press it,' he urged. 'Now you have a motorised roller blade.' I looked at the button suspiciously. 'What if it runs away with me?' I asked, and he shook his head no. 'See, this is for accelerating,' and he pointed to a handle. Slowly, I pressed the button, scared that I would be run away with. Instead, there was only a gentle humming sound. Then the green man pointed to the handle and said, 'If you push it this way, you'll move faster. If you push like this, you'll go slower.' I tried it. It worked. I was comfortable in seconds. I loved going fast. 'Whee!' I screamed as I whizzed along the path. Daddu, your grandfather, could hardly keep up with me, I was going so fast. After I understood how it worked, I stopped. The green man was fluttering his wings. 'Carry your house with you, huh?' he was saying to himself. 'I wonder if I can carry my house with me and use my wings. I'll have to come up with something.' Then he looked at me and asked, 'All well with your roller blade?' I was thrilled with my roller blade. Your grandfather was looking rather green, maybe because he was jealous. But I was thrilled.

"The green man kept saying, 'I really like the idea of carrying a house along. Well, it's time to go home and see what I can do. Won't be simple to make a home that I can take with me. But you've given me a lovely idea. I hope your day decides to wake up tomorrow. Enjoy your roller blade,' and with that he fluttered away, a bright green and pink thing in the sky. Daddu, your grandfather, and I started towards home, and we were there in seconds. I accelerated, and Daddu jumped along saying, 'Oh, now we can really have adventures together.' I had been thinking I was now going to have my adventures alone! After all, I was going faster than your grandfather. But we did have adventures together. We went to Old Delhi together. I've been there, Padu, I've been there with your grandfather." And Kachhua took a long satisfied drag of his pipe and slowly let out perfect circles of smoke.

Everybody was looking at Kachhua in amazement. What a story! Then Padu said, "Where is your roller blade now?" Kachhua answered, "It was stolen. Some years ago, it was stolen. These things happen when you have something fancy. Another kachhua must have taken it, I guess. I hope. It wouldn't be much use to anyone else. Oh, we'd had fun by the time it was stolen. We'd been to Old Delhi by then." Nobody said anything more for a while. Then Lulu, in her small voice, said, "What a lovely story, Kachhua. Tell me, did the green man ever get to carry his house with him?" "That

I don't know," answered Kachhua. "I never met him again. I hope he did. It's special to have your house with you. In fact, I'm off for a nap now." He tapped his pipe empty, and within seconds there was only a round, brown shell sitting under the arbi. "Siesta time," said Padu the daddu and hopped away just as Lulu and Arbi shrunk up for a nap, imagining what fun it must have been to be on a roller blade, and thinking how nice it would be to have your own shell to crawl away and into any time you wanted!

Mannoo the Monkey and his Hat

The monkey put on his hat and looked at himself. He liked what he saw. His top hat suited him, he thought. How lucky he had been to have found Naresh's grandfather's room open all those years ago. Naresh's grandfather lived on the roof, in the single room up there that had been built for him. His *barsati* was quite modest. Mannoo, the monkey, had seen quite a few more elaborate ones. But Naresh's grandfather was a spare man. His barsati was just like him. The room was large with a single bed and a side table in it. Opposite the bed were two small armchairs, with a long table in front of them. On one side of the room was a small desk and a chair that fit under the desk. The curtains on the windows were plain. Cream-coloured, they got dirty in the dust quickly, and Naresh's grandfather always scolded the washerwoman when he wanted the curtains removed and washed. Even if she did everything just right, he scolded her.

Naresh's grandfather's bedroom also had a cupboard. The solid Godrej cupboard had several keys to it. Naresh's grandfather used all of them. He would lock the cupboard every time after he opened it. First he would fit one key in, and turn it and turn it. Mannoo heard the key clicking and clicking. Then Naresh's grandfather took this key out and inserted a second one. He did the same thing. Then he used a third key and clicked and clicked. After that, he would push the handle down and open the cupboard to take out or put in what he needed. Then he would shut the cupboard and start turning keys in the locks one after another. Naresh's grandfather did this even if he only wanted to put in or take out a cotton shirt or a *lungi*. Even for one ironed white handkerchief, Naresh's grandfather turned all the keys in the lock. The room had no other furniture. There were no pictures on the walls and no carpets on the floor. But there was a top hat. On top of the cupboard, on a piece of plastic that lay on a sheet of newspaper, was the top hat. Naresh's grandfather put it there when he came back home after his evening out. Then he placed a white muslin cloth over the top hat so it wouldn't get dusty.

There was nothing extra about Naresh's grandfather like there was nothing extra in his room. Tall and thin, he looked like the simple stick he used for walking. His bones were pointy and seemed to want to come out of the skin on his arms and on his face. Mannoo had never seen Naresh's grandfather's legs, so he didn't know if the bones wanted to come out of his knees as well. Naresh's grandfather had no hair at all. His head was shaped like a well-rounded egg. His glasses were round and plain. His teeth were false and straight. Usually, Naresh's grandfather sat in his room without his teeth in his mouth. Then his lips would get sucked inside his mouth, and they would look wrinkly. When he put his teeth in, which he did whenever he

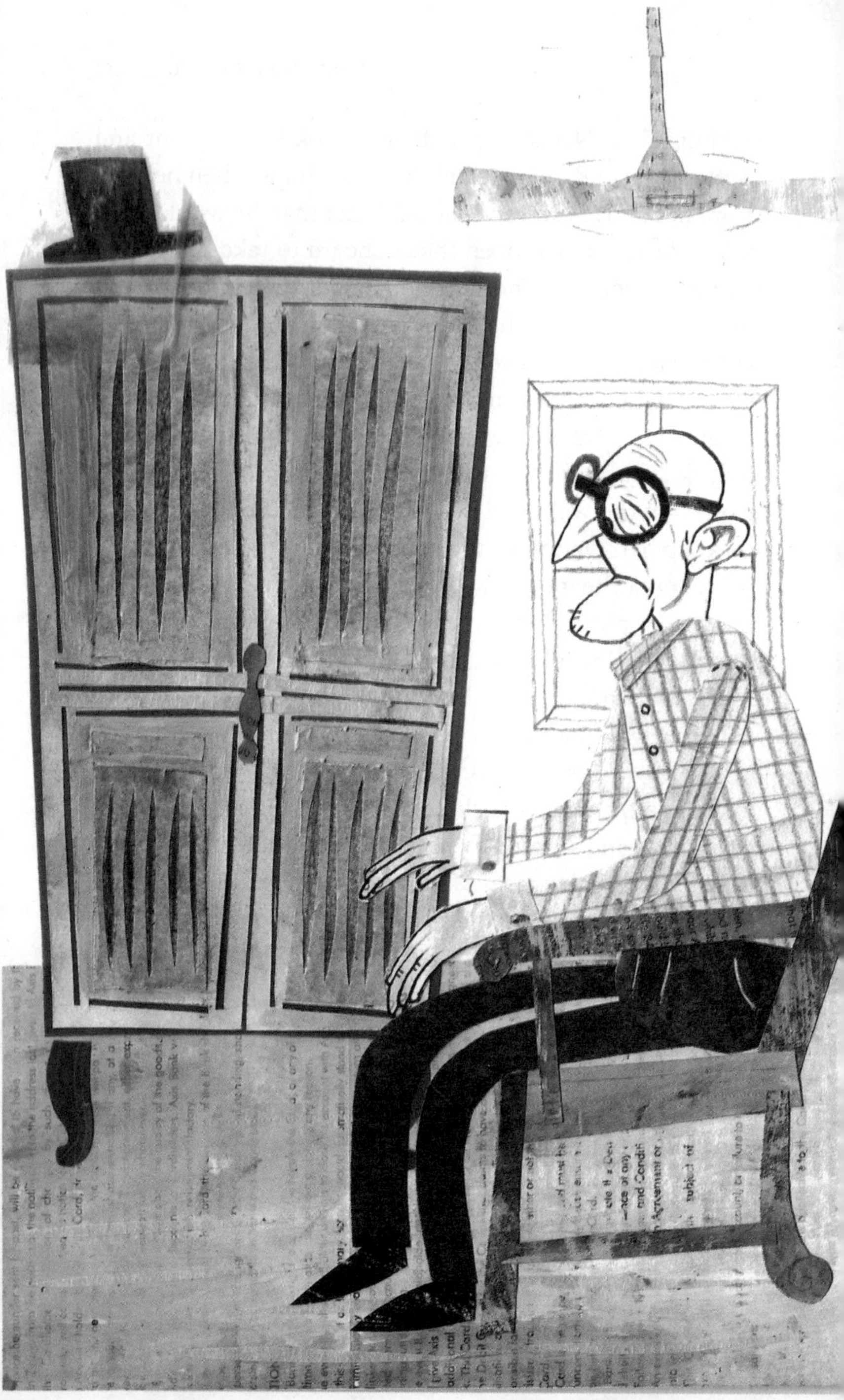

went out or when he was getting ready to eat, his lips got tighter, and his mouth came out of where it had been hiding.

Every morning, Naresh's grandfather made his own tea in the small kitchen also on the roof. Although the kitchen was not attached to Naresh's grandfather's bedroom, it was his. There he had a small gas range and a tiny fridge. The only thing he made there was his bed tea, unless he was in a grumpy mood. If he were angry with his son's family who lived downstairs, where Naresh's grandfather ate all his meals, he would insist on making his own soup in the kitchen. He always made a mess of the soup. Somehow he spilled it on the counter, and Mannoo was so glad for that. Droppings of Maggi soup decorated the counter after Naresh's grandfather had made his dinner. He would take his soup and go into his room to sip it watching the news on his new Sony television. He would leave the kitchen door unlocked, because he was going to bring his bowl back and wash it in the little sink in the kitchen. Only then would he lock the kitchen for the night. Mannoo, who lived behind the water tank on top of the roof of the room on the roof, would have smelled the mushroom or chicken or sweet corn soup boiling. He would wait for his moment and come slinking down to the roof as soon as Naresh's grandfather went into his bedroom. If Mannoo was very lucky, he could even get some soup out of the saucepan on the stove. That didn't happen too often because Naresh's grandfather also liked his soup. When he made it, he usually poured all of it into a deep bowl his granddaughter, Tanya, had brought him from America. The bowl said, "The World's Best Grandpa" all around its beige and pink-striped roundness. Naresh's grandfather did not look like the world's best grandpa. Mannoo thought he might be the world's worst grandpa, he was so grumpy. But Mannoo didn't care about that. It wasn't his grandpa!

And he had a top hat that he had brought back with him on the boat that brought him back from London many, many years ago, when he had finished studying for his medical exams. Mannoo knew all about this top hat. His own grandfather, who was the world's best grandpa, although he had no cup to tell him that, had told him about the top hat. He had told him stories of how Naresh's grandfather, as a dashing young man in a top hat and a walking stick, would stroll along the grassy paths in Lodhi Gardens in the evenings. He would tip his hat to people he knew, and otherwise he would walk straight and look neither to the left nor to the right. If he had looked to the left, he would have seen the tombs. If he had looked to the right, he would have seen Mannoo's grandfather hanging from one tree or another, perhaps from the gulmohar or perhaps the jacaranda, depending on his mood. In the summers, if he had looked to the left or to the right, he might have seen Mannoo's grandfather sniffing the gardenia bushes. Mannoo's grandfather could never resist burrowing into the dark green leaves of the gardenia, breathing in the scent of the heavy white flowers, a scent that made Mannoo's grandfather long for something, although he couldn't say what.

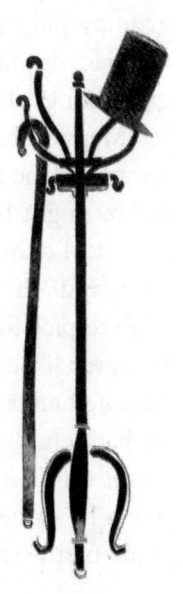

After Naresh's grandfather had walked the whole outer round of Lodhi Gardens, he would return to his car. The driver would hold the door open for him. Naresh's grandfather had to take off his top hat to get into the car. He would place the hat on the seat next to him as the driver sped him to the Gymkhana Club. There, Naresh's grandfather played two hands of bridge and drank two whisky sodas. His top hat and walking stick were placed on the hat stand that was in the bridge room. Nobody spoke to Naresh's grandfather, and he spoke to no one. Nobody in the card room spoke at all. They only nodded their heads to each other and settled down to play. The waiters knew just what drinks everyone wanted and how many they wanted. The waiters brought the drinks and placed them quietly on the table so the bridge players could concentrate. Mannoo's grandfather liked the club, and when Mannoo was tiny, his grandfather often took him there for the evening. The large neem trees of the club were amongst the best in all of Delhi. The mango trees were as lovely. Tall and thick, the trees shaded the gardens of the club and allowed parrots, squirrels, snakes, caterpillars, sparrows, crows and monkeys to live in their branches. Hanging from the branches of these trees, Mannoo and his grandfather could peer into the card room and see everything going on inside. When Naresh's grandfather lost his game, they knew it before he came out wearing a frown beneath his top hat. They had already seen him say something mean to his partner, and they had seen him slam his glass of whisky down on the table, push his chair back so that it almost toppled over, and walk out in a huff.

That had happened a long time ago. Mannoo's grandfather had died many, many years ago. Naresh's grandfather had died many, many years ago as well, but not before Mannoo stole his top hat. He had not meant to. He was fond of the grumpy old man, just because he was so used to him. He was part of Mannoo's family, after all, even though Naresh's grandfather always raised his stick at him if he happened to see Mannoo hanging on the roof. Mannoo, of course, was always on the roof. He was either leaving it or returning to it. He might have gone out for a jaunt, or he might have gone to Lodhi Gardens to smell the gardenia and think of his grandfather, or he might have gone to the Gymkhana Club to pick food off the plates of unsuspecting guests. But he never liked to be away from home for long. He always returned after a jaunt to make sure that everything was as he had left it. It always was. Mannoo had learnt long ago that it was best for nobody to know where he lived. So, even when he came to his own roof, to the roof on top of the room on the roof, he did so slyly. First he always went to the neighbour's roof. Luckily, nobody used that roof, so Mannoo didn't have to fear being chased or stoned. From that roof Mannoo would creep to his own little space, looking around him all the time to make sure nobody saw him. He knew that if Naresh's family found out he lived on their roof, even if it was the roof on top of the roof, they would run him away. After Mannoo had come home, he would wait for the best moment to go to the main roof of the house to see what was going on there.

Usually, he would manage to get some food. Often, mangoes would be drying on the roof, or the cauliflower, just washed for *achar*, would be sunning itself. Mannoo would manage nice handfuls of fruits and vegetables, if he were lucky. If he wasn't lucky, and that happened as well, he would find no food on the roof, but he would find other things. Once he found a small ball that had landed there from some children playing on the street. Naresh's grandfather refused to return the ball to the children and scolded them for being reckless and dangerous. But he had left the ball where it had landed, and Mannoo had picked it up later for himself. Another time Mannoo found a wire basket on the roof. He couldn't understand how it got there, but he was glad to have it. The basket was pink, and you could hang it from the hook on the top. Mannoo hung it as soon as he found it. First he thought he would keep his ball there, but then he realised the crows would steal it. So Mannoo hid the ball under the water tank on the roof and kept the basket empty. He liked to see it sway in the breeze with its pretty pink wires. But the best thing that Mannoo had found on the roof had been Naresh's grandfather's top hat. Well, Mannoo had not technically found the hat on the roof. No, he had taken the top hat from inside Naresh's grandfather's room, from its safe spot on top of the Godrej cupboard and from under its white muslin veil. But he had not planned to do so. It had just happened, as things do.

Sometimes Mannoo thought his grandfather would not have been happy to hear that he had taken the top hat. Mannoo's grandfather had always taught him to treasure the family that he lived with. "Even if they don't know you're with them, it doesn't matter," he had said to Mannoo. "You know you're with them. That's what matters." Mannoo had nodded when he heard that. He believed that. He liked the family that he lived with. Yet, when the chance came, he had taken the top hat. It had not been easy, and Mannoo had been very, very lucky. Naresh's grandfather never, ever left the door of his room unlocked. Whenever he left it, even if he was going only to the kitchen, he pulled the door shut and bolted the large iron bolt outside. He always did that. Except once, when Naresh's grandfather had been so surprised that he forgot, and Mannoo had been so lucky that he had seen his chance and taken it.

It was early on a Sunday morning in spring. The peepul had just put out its new leaves and was showing off its pretty green colour to the rising sun. The parrots were dashing in and out of the green leaves, busy at their game of hide and seek. Mannoo was wondering who could ever seek the birds, they were so well hidden in the green peepul. Yet, they were at it, and they were chirruping loudly. Any snake in that tree, and it will run away, thought Mannoo to himself as he slowly stretched out his sleepy arms and his sleepy legs and his sleepy tail. Those parrots give you a headache, Mannoo was thinking even as he was deciding what to do for the day. All of a sudden, there was a new commotion.

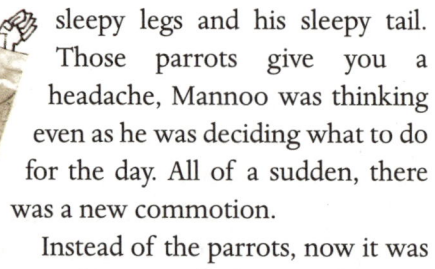

Instead of the parrots, now it was Naresh's grandfather making a big noise. Mannoo heard some furniture crash, followed by sounds of a scuffle, and then he heard Naresh's grandfather scream, "Get away from here or I will kill you!" This was followed by the sound of Naresh's grandfather's stick being beaten against something. First it sounded like the floor. Then it sounded like the wall. Then it might have been the table. But Mannoo could not understand why Naresh's grandfather should beat the floor, and the wall, and the table. How could they have upset him? Mannoo decided to stop being lazy and peep down below him to see what he could see. As he did so, Naresh's grandfather came running out of his room. He looked crumpled in a white *kurta* and a lungi, and he was holding his stick out in front of him and beating it wildly here and there. "Get away!" he was screaming and throwing the stick out to this side and that. By now he was on the roof, lunging after something that Mannoo could not see. What was upsetting Naresh's grandfather so much? As far as Mannoo could make out, he was beating the stick in the air.

From downstairs came the sounds of steps. Naresh's father and mother were standing breathless on the roof. Both were crumpled as well, probably because they had just been woken up by Naresh's grandfather's noise. "What's the matter, Papa?" asked Naresh's father. "What are you doing beating your stick in the air?" "Don't be a fool," roared Naresh's grandfather, "I am not beating the air. I am beating a snake that's in my room. A poisonous one at that, I'm sure," and he continued beating the air. Naresh's mother screamed "A snake, a snake!" and ran back downstairs. Naresh's father went up to his father and tried to hold his flailing hand. "Come, Papa," he said kindly, "you go downstairs and I'll find the snake. Come," and he started leading his father down the stairs.

Naresh's grandfather was so upset by the events that he allowed himself to be led downstairs. He used his stick to take first one step and then the next, and he leaned on his son who held the elbow of the arm without the stick. Mannoo was laughing up there on the roof of the room on the roof. He had been right, he was thinking, all those chattering parrots had drawn the snakes out of the tree. The snakes must've eaten a few, of course, but they were more bothered by the noise, it seemed. And now those snakes were in Naresh's grandfather's room. What a way to wake up on a Sunday morning, he was thinking, when it suddenly dawned on him: the room was open. In fact, the door was wide open. He had never been inside this room that was right beneath him. He had only peeped in from the window, hanging on the tiger palm that grew tall outside the window. Here was his chance to go inside the room. He had to take a quick peek inside the room. Mannoo could not resist. And he had to watch out for snakes. He hated snakes as much as Naresh's grandfather did.

Mannoo quickly swung down the roof and peeked into the room. He saw the unmade bed, the armchairs, and the table. Things were crooked from all the crashing around that Naresh's grandfather had done. Mannoo looked at the wall. There was no snake. He looked on the floor and could not see one there, either. Then he looked on the bed, and there he did see one. It was pink and brown. It seemed to like nestling in the soft white sheet and the *razai* on the bed. Mannoo quickly looked behind him. Nobody was there. He looked to the left and to the right. Nobody was there. Before he went into the room, he decided he was going to behave as if he was in charge. He cleared his throat and entered the room. From the doorway he said, "Snake, do you think because the parrots are noisy you should come and disturb other people's Sunday mornings?" The snake looked up surprised. He had been so content to burrow into the softness of Naresh's grandfather's bed. He had been hoping he could sleep a little longer since the parrots had woken him up so early and so rudely. He lifted his head up from the razai and asked in a surly voice, "And who might you be?" Mannoo had to think quickly. He had to be somebody important or the snake would tell him to get out. So Mannoo said, "I'm part of the family. My family has been with the family for generations." Mannoo was not lying. Even though Naresh's family didn't know it, he was part of the family, just as his grandfather had been. After saying his bit, Mannoo looked at the snake to see how it would respond. Mannoo was standing tall: he had puffed out his chest, his clever face was looking cleverer, and he had put his hands behind him. Mannoo was sure he looked important. The snake's response surprised him. "Whatever," it said and burrowed right back into bed.

Mannoo stood in the doorway feeling a bit foolish. Now what should he do? Should he enter the room to look around and pretend there was no snake snoozing in bed, or should he leave? Mannoo decided to ignore the snake. He came into the room, and he first walked to the desk. There he picked up Naresh's grandfather's jar of pens. Then he put them down. Then he lifted the lamp on the table, and he dropped it as he was putting it down. The noise woke the snake, who lifted his head up lazily and looked at Mannoo. Mannoo looked back, trying to bring that important look back on his face. The snake slumped back onto the bed. Now Mannoo had moved to the other side of the room. He was near the Godrej cupboard and could not resist trying the handle, just in case it was open. It wasn't. So Mannoo turned away from the cupboard forlornly, knowing he would never look into it. As he did so, he saw the snake looking at him again. The creak of the metal handle must've disturbed it. Now the snake said, "I think you're a thief, or why are you picking things up and dropping them, and trying to open locked cupboards?"

And that's when Mannoo had the idea. He had crept towards the door and had just noticed the muslin-draped top hat on top of the Godrej. "I have come here to get this hat," he said importantly, leaping to the top of the cupboard for it. "Naresh's grandfather needs it and you've run him out of his room." With that, Mannoo whisked the muslin off the hat, but not before he let out a pitiful scream. On top of the hat, on top of the muslin that draped the hat, lay another lazy snake. He was fast asleep, so he hadn't seen Mannoo at all. Luckily, or Mannoo would've been bitten by the snake. As it was, everything happened so fast that the hat was in Mannoo's hands before he had fully realised that he'd seen another snake. He jumped down from the cupboard, glared at the snake on the bed, and ran out of the room. In a second, he was back up on his own roof. He made it just in time, for moments later, noises of men coming up the stairs could be heard. After that, Mannoo heard large sticks being beaten here and there and lots of feet stomping before everything was quiet at last.

Naresh's grandfather stayed downstairs after that. First, the family wanted to be sure that they had found all the snakes that had come into the room. Naresh's grandfather said he himself had seen three. The family wondered how many more there could be. During this time, Naresh's grandfather didn't go out. He never even came to the roof. In fact, the event seemed to change him. Suddenly, instead of being tall and straight, he became short and bent. His hands started shaking and he started complaining that his knees hurt walking up the stairs. Naresh's father said that his father should now live downstairs. He thought he was too old to be up on the roof by himself. Naresh's grandfather seemed to agree because the room upstairs got locked, and nobody came to it anymore.

Mannoo was sorry about how things had gone with Naresh's grandfather, even though he was so grumpy. He had been fond of the grumpy old man, just because he was family. But Mannoo was thrilled that he'd managed to get Naresh's grandfather's top hat before the room was locked up. Mannoo would put on the hat every evening. He behaved as if he was Naresh's grandfather, with the only difference being that he was a monkey, and so he didn't play bridge at the club and he didn't have a driver. But every evening, Mannoo put on his top hat (luckily it fit him perfectly, as if it had been made for him) and he would go for a scamper in Lodhi Gardens. He leapt from the gulmohar to the jacaranda trees, and in the summers he nestled into the gardenia with his top hat on his head. The smell of the gardenia made him long for something, but he didn't know what. Then he would go to the Delhi Gymkhana Club and settle into the broad branches of a mango tree that grew near the swimming pool. The younger monkeys would go and steal kebabs for him and the other elders, so Mannoo usually had an excellent dinner. Then he would go home and place the top hat in the pink wire basket that hung in his little space on the roof above the room on the roof. Mannoo covered the top hat with a thick cloth, so the sun wouldn't bleach it and so the crows wouldn't come and try to eat it.

Just once Mannoo felt sad that he had taken Naresh's grandfather's top hat. It was years after he had done so. Naresh's grandfather was now nothing like he used to be. Even though he was still thin, he looked as if he was a lot of nubby rounded things that wrapped around each other. His granddaughter, Tanya, was getting married. She had come back from America with cups for her mother, her father and her brother, Naresh. They said, "The World's Best Mother," "The World's Best Father," and "# 1 Brother". Naresh's mother's cup was red, his father's was black, and Naresh's was brown. Tanya's husband was a small Jewish boy with pink cheeks and dark curly hair. Naresh's grandfather was not happy about the marriage, but he didn't say anything because there were so many things he wasn't happy about. If he was to start speaking, he would have to go on for a long time.

He wanted to wear his top hat for the wedding. "Oh no, Papa," groaned his son when Naresh's grandfather asked him to go upstairs to his room and get his hat. "Papa, you can't wear that hat. You have to wear a *pagdi*. You can't wear that top hat." Naresh's grandfather insisted at first, saying he had to wear his top hat because he was a doctor who had trained in England just as the servant came down and said there was no hat on top of the Godrej. So, Naresh's father just plopped a pink pagdi, that had been tied earlier, on his father's head, just like that. Naresh's grandfather had by now forgotten about his top hat. He didn't notice what was on his head, and he just walked where he was led by his son. Mannoo was glad to see that. He missed his own grandfather, and he knew he would have missed him more if Naresh's grandfather had really missed his top hat. Then Mannoo thought if he hadn't stolen the top hat, it would be old and musty and dusty by now, and perhaps some rats would've chewed on it to amuse themselves. It was a good thing he had taken that top hat. He had given it a new life.

The Red Shoe

Once upon a time there was a little Irish elf who lived in Cambodia. How did he get there? Oh, that's a long story and another story. This one is about the shoes he made—little red shoes, big red shoes, red shoes with straps and red shoes with laces, red shoes with heels and red shoes without, red shoes with large eyes and pointy noses, and red shoes with small eyes and flat noses. The shoes were of soft leather and hard leather, and they shone and didn't. Whichever kind of shoe you wanted was there. Well, almost. The funny thing about these shoes was that there was only one of each, and each was a left shoe.

In the elf's workshop, rows and rows of shoes stood neatly by size, shape, and shine, and they were all left shoes. There he displayed the small shoes and the large shoes, the shiny shoes and the un-shiny shoes. People saw the shoes and exclaimed, "My, look at those lovely shoes!" and came closer to look. They picked up a shoe or two or three, and then they realised that something was odd. So they asked the elf, "Where's the other shoe?" and the elf always answered, "Which other shoe?" So the shoppers asked again, "The shoe for the other foot," and the elf shook his head sadly and said, "These are all the shoes I have." He seemed not to understand that people needed two shoes not one, that people needed a shoe for the left foot and for the right one.

One day, a small boy was walking in the market with his mother. "Oh, Mama, look," he exclaimed when he saw the rows upon rows of red shoes. "Look at those shiny shoes. I want one, I want one, I want one," he said, dancing round and round his mother. "And one shoe you will get," muttered his mother as she took in the fact that she was staring at rows of left shoes. She picked up the shoe her boy was pointing to and said to the elf, "May I see the shoe for the other foot, please?" "Which other foot?" asked the elf, bewildered. "The shoe for the other foot, obviously," said the mother, pointing down to her own two feet in scuffed black shoes. "Left foot, left shoe; right foot, right shoe," she repeated as she held up first her left and then her right foot for the elf to see.

She was pleased with herself; she was doing the elf a favour, she thought, by making him understand that people needed not one shoe but two. To her surprise, the elf curled up his nose and said as he turned away, "What ugly, ugly shoes!" He started dusting and polishing the shoes he displayed. The mother was annoyed. It's true her shoes were old and needed a polish, but at least she had two. "You are a fool," she said to the elf. "No wonder nobody buys your shoes." "Who says nobody buys my shoes?" asked the elf, although the woman was telling the truth and the elf knew it. "Who buys your shoes?" asked the woman. "Who would buy just one shoe?" "This little boy will," said the elf, because he could see that the little boy still held the left shoe he had selected when he first stopped at the store.

"Absolutely not," said the woman. "My son is certainly not buying a single shoe." But she had it wrong. The little boy refused to put the shoe down. "I wannit, I wannit, I wannit," he started screaming, clutching the shoe. "It's my shoe, itsmyshoe, itsmyshoe," he repeated even as he kicked his mother who was trying to pry the shoe away. "You will not buy that shoe," screamed his mother, but she needn't have bothered. Sometimes, her son, young T. GuruArath, could decide just what he wanted, and no amount of talking, caressing, cajoling, or bribing would make him change his mind. Soon Guru was on the floor, the shoe clutched to his chest. He was beating his feet and kicking up quite a whirl of dust, and he was beating his head and creating a little cloud of dust there as well. Loud sobs and screams accompanied this performance, and a small crowd of interested people had gathered to see what the commotion was about. "My, I wonder what that mother has done to that poor boy," said a woman and others started murmuring similar things.

GuruArath's mother was embarrassed and said in a small, irritated voice, "How much is this shoe?" The elf answered evenly, "One hundred dollars only." "What?" exclaimed the mother. "That's outrageous!" But the elf had seen his advantage. "You don't have to buy it," he said, knowing fully well that the mother had no hope of leaving the shop with her son if she didn't buy the shoe. She quietly took the money out and said, "Guru, let the man pack the shoe." But Guru shook his head and refused. "My shoe," he said, "it's my shoe." "Yes," said his mother, "it's only going to be packed so you can carry it home safely." Again, Guru refused, and repeated, "My shoe, my shoe!" He was standing up proudly now, holding the shoe in his hand. The elf took the money and put it away as the woman glared at him while taking her son away. "Come back soon," said the elf to the boy who was nodding yes even as the mother was pulling the boy away, muttering, "Stupid scene, stupid shoe."

Mama was worried. What was she going to do with this silly shoe once Guru had outgrown his passion for it? She was sure he would throw it away as soon as they got home. Then her husband would see the shoe, hear the whole story, and reprove her for handling Guru's tantrum just as they had decided they shouldn't—by giving in. Mama was morose. She had wasted money, she had let her son see that if he kicked and screamed and yelled in a public place, he could quickly become her boss, and she was in for a lecture. So she said to her young boy, "Why don't you wear the shoe?" just so she could demonstrate how silly he'd been. "Okay," said Guru obligingly and stopped on the side of the street to change his shoe.

After he had done so, he looked a fool. On the left foot he had on a shiny, new, red shoe. On the right, he had on his old, scruffy, once-white-now-grey sneaker. It didn't look right. This was not the way to treat a new red shoe, even Guru could see, and so he removed his right sneaker and looked down again. Not much better. Now the shiny red shoe was paired with a crumpled, sweaty, once-white-now-grey sock. And so Guru took off his sock as well. Then he handed both sneakers and socks to his mother while perching on one foot. His mother was watching him to see what he would do next. He, of course, was not going to admit that he'd been a fool to demand a single shoe. Guru, she knew, was going to hop along on one foot as if it was the most normal thing in the world.

She was right. Guru hopped. He hopped again. He hopped yet again. After each hop he stopped, as if he wanted to see what his mother would do when he stopped. His mother did nothing. She merely said, "Let's hop faster, Guru. Home is still some distance away." Guru hopped faster. And then a funny thing happened. He had stopped hopping; he knew he had stopped hopping after four or five quick hops, yet his body kept hopping along, even though he had stopped it. Hop, hop, hop, he went, and although he meant to stop, he didn't stop. His mind said he'd stopped, but he could see he hadn't. His mother was running to keep up with him and said, "Stop showing off, Guru." He shook his head from side to side and said, "Ma, I'm not showing off. I'm not even hopping, honest." Ma groaned. "Oh Guru, haven't you put me through enough for today? Why are you lying now when

I can see you hopping?" But Guru couldn't even hear her. He had hopped so far away that he'd passed the door to his own house and had barely noticed his surprised father in the front yard staring at a little exclamation mark—a blur of white with a drop of red—that had whizzed past. "What's that?" Pa asked his wife as she came running, holding Guru's sneakers. "Where's Guru? Why are you running? Why are his sneakers in your hands?" Ma didn't answer. She collapsed in the front garden, heaving strongly, and put her head in her hands.

"What's the matter, why won't you talk?" begged Pa, as he came over to her and sat down in the grass. "That was Guru," said the tired mother. "That little, speedy thing that whizzed past was your son Guru, hopping on one foot in a shiny red shoe." Pa looked at his wife in sympathy, but he was shaking his head. "Wife, what are you saying? How can our son hop so fast? And he doesn't have a pair of red shoes." "No, he doesn't," said his wife, "but he does have one red shoe. And it has hopped away with him, hasn't it?" Pa was still looking sympathetically at Ma. She snapped, "Oh, stop it, T, I'm not mad. No, the sun hasn't affected me. I'm telling you the truth." Pa continued to look doubtful, but he was thinking hard. What could he say or do next to really get the truth out of his wife? After all, his son was missing, wasn't he?

"Let's start at the beginning," he said, asking his wife to repeat everything just as it had occurred. She did, but she did make Guru's tantrum even more dramatic than it had been. Not only did she have to justify spending so much money on one shoe, but she also had to justify an absent son! She finished her tale, put her head back in her arms, and sobbed,

"My son, my son. Where has he gone?" Pa comforted her. He held her and soothed her and stroked her hair and kissed her head. He was so busy calming Mama, and Mama was so busy crying, that neither noticed the exclamation mark with the red dot enter the garden and settle down next to them, now looking more like a robust question mark. Guru immediately took the red shoe off and pushing it into his father's hands, said, "Look, Pa, look what Ma bought me." Both parents screamed in delight at the sound of Guru's voice. Ma immediately hugged him, and Guru restrained himself from squirming out of her embrace when he saw her tear-stained face. "Where have you been?" both parents asked at once. "Why did you rush off like that?" said Ma. "I'm sure your foot is sore and your leg must hurt from all that hopping."

Guru sat quiet for a while and then answered, "Ma, Pa, there's something odd in this shoe. I promise, Ma, I wasn't hopping. Remember I told you I wasn't hopping. See, I had stopped. I didn't want to hop after the first few hops. My leg was tired. So I stopped. But I hadn't stopped. The foot wanted to keep going, I guess, and I couldn't do anything about it. That's why I couldn't say hello, Pa. My foot and shoe just ran away with me. They took me all the way down to the dumpster at the end of the colony, and then they made me dance around the dumpster. Then I thought we were going on the highway, but the shoe seemed to change its mind suddenly. I have no idea why we turned around, but we did, and I'm so glad. I was so scared. The shoe was hopping slower now, again I don't know why. I had no control over it. It brought me back here, and I took it off as soon as I could. I don't want to wear this shoe any more. It scares me."

Ma, Pa and Guru stared down at the innocent-looking red shoe. It was still shining, despite all the places it had been. "It's a nice looking shoe," said Pa. "I can see why you'd want it," he added, making both Guru and Ma feel better. Then he made Guru feel worse by saying, "But Guru, I am tired of your tall tales. You wore this shoe and hopped away on it just to scare us. No shoe hops on its own. A person hops. You hopped. No, we've had enough nonsense for one day, and your mother is exhausted. Go inside, wash your hands and feet, and let's have some dinner. After that we'll decide how you should be punished for scaring your mother and me." "T, we also have to punish him for that tantrum," added Ma. She knew you couldn't let children get away with tantrums without punishing them. Guru looked crestfallen. "I'm telling you the truth," he said, but nobody heard him. Instead, his father sternly said, "I told you to go and get ready for dinner, Guru."

Guru stood up. Very slowly, he put his left foot back into the red shoe. The shoe fit him perfectly. It was shiny, with a nice round nose and flashy eyes. The tongue of the shoe was ridged and long and lay comfortably on his foot. This shoe certainly looked as if it had been made for him. Instinctively, Guru folded his right leg and hopped on his left foot. Hop. Stop. Hop. Stop. Slowly he made his way to the house. Every time he stopped, the shoe stopped with him. This time, there was no confusion between what his mind decided and what his foot wanted. Hop. Stop. Once Guru was inside the house, he stared at the stairs. Hopping up the stairs would be hard, he thought. As it was, his spirits were flagging. He had wanted to show his parents that the shoe hopped when it wanted and not when Guru wanted. Yet, the shoe had been utterly obedient. Not once had it hopped without instructions.

Guru decided to hop up the stairs. Hop, he went, up the first stair. Hop, he went, up the second stair. This is slow, he was thinking to himself, when it happened. All of a sudden, he went hop, hop, hop, hop, and found himself at the very top of the stairs in a jiffy. His parents had seen him whiz up the stairs. "See, you're doing it again," they both said in unison. There was no point in Guru saying anything. So, he didn't, and went to his room, now slow hop by slow hop, where he took the shoe off. He held it up and said, "You're a funny shoe. You're magic, aren't you?" There was no answer from the shoe. But by now Guru knew the shoe had a mind of its own, and he didn't like it. He certainly didn't like the idea of a shoe with its own mind on his left foot. This shoe wasn't worth having, he decided. But what was he to do with it? Throw it, return it, gift it? Kill it by cutting it up? Guru couldn't decide. Besides, Ma was calling him downstairs for dinner already.

Guru left the shoe where it was and washed up as he'd been told to do. Then he walked down for dinner looking quite puzzled and preoccupied. At the end of dinner, Pa said, "Guru, here are your punishments: for lying to us about hopping, you will have to clear the table for two weeks. For the tantrum you threw, no television for one week. Now come and give your daddy a goodnight kiss." The last thing Guru felt like doing was kissing his father, but he obliged. A small slur landed on Pa's cheek as Guru moved away from his father as soon as he could. Then Guru said, "I don't want the shoe in my room." Ma and Pa looked at him in amazement. "Why ever not?" said Ma. "You're going to have the shoe in your room, after you made me spend all that good money on that silly shoe." "No, Ma, please," begged Guru. "That shoe does what it wants." "Don't be silly, Guru, it's a shoe. Shoes don't do what they want." "This one does, Ma, honest, this one does. It hopped me up the stairs, didn't you see?" "Yes, I saw you zoom-hopping up the stairs, but the shoe didn't hop you up. You hopped the shoe up. Shoes aren't alive. You are. You decided what you're doing." Guru could only shake his head. His parents didn't understand.

After finishing his chores, Guru went upstairs to bed. He had decided to place the shoe outside on the balcony. He found an old shoebox and picked up the red shoe to place it in, saying, "Here you are, Shoe. Out you go." "Please don't put me out," said the shoe. Guru was startled. "You talk?" he said, in surprise. "Yes," replied the shoe. "Please don't put me out. I didn't mean to hurt you. I just wanted you to see how special I am. You can do all sorts of fun things with me, promise." Guru wasn't convinced. "You were dangerous, scary, frightening and mean," said Guru. "Yes," admitted the shoe. "I was. You know how it can be sometimes. One just gets in the mood to be a bit, y'know, nasty-ish. Well, like you were with your ma in the shop. Poor lady. Everybody thought she was a mean and nasty mother because you were making such a fuss. See, I misbehaved, too, just as you did. But I won't anymore. Now I'm your shoe, and I'll work just for you. You'll have the best adventures hopping with me, I promise you."

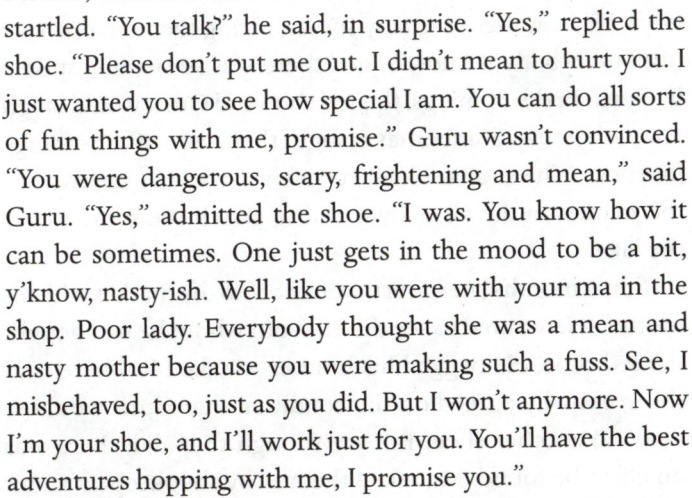

"Hmm…." Guru considered the offer. He could get to school in a jiffy and travel to all sorts of strange places with this shoe. He could become the most popular boy in the school with this shoe. And the shoe was right. Guru had behaved badly in the store with his mother just as the shoe had behaved badly with him. So Guru said, "Okay. It's a deal. I'll trust you. I won't put you out or chop you up or throw you away or take you back, but only if you'll work with me and for me. Agreed?" The shoe flapped its tongue readily and said repeatedly, "Agreed, agreed. Oh, what fun we'll have. You'll enjoy me, really, you will. I knew that from the minute you selected me. You knew that, too. That's why you wanted me, even though there's only one of me. I'm so glad you bought me." Now Guru started feeling glad as well. He felt he could trust the shoe, and he looked forward to many, many adventures with it.

And that's just what happened. Guru and the red shoe had a wonderful time. Guru hopped to school and impressed the boys. He beat them at many sports, racing them on one foot until everybody acknowledged there was something special in Guru. In the evenings, the red shoe and Guru would laugh about their day. Sometimes at night they went off on strange journeys. The shoe took Guru safely across the highway to the market in the next town and to watch the sunrise over the lake.

Some months later, Guru went back to the market with his mother. He wanted to see the elf from whom he had bought the red shoe. He begged his mother to take him there, and she eventually agreed on the condition that Guru wouldn't demand another shoe. But try though they did, there was no elf to be found. Ma asked the nearby shopkeepers about the elf, but nobody had heard about him or seen him— ever. Ma spoke of the red shoes in neat little rows, and the shopkeepers looked at her strangely. Eventually, one gruff man said, "Nobody here ever sold red shoes, ma'am. Certainly we would never have a mad cobbler in our market who would make and sell only left shoes." So Ma and Guru left the market. They knew better, of course. "See, Ma," said Guru, "I told you there was magic in the shoes. A magic elf sold me a magic shoe." Ma just scratched her head and looked at her son. She wouldn't say he was right, but at the same time there was clearly something funny going on.

When Guru and Ma got home, she asked her son if she could see his red shoe. "Why?" asked Guru. His mother didn't bother answering him and instead just repeated her instruction: "Get me your red shoe." Guru climbed up to his room slowly. When he got there, he told the red shoe what had happened in the market and what his mother now wanted. The red shoe listened and didn't say a word. After Guru had finished, the shoe said, "Ready? Let's go." In the drawing room, where his mother was sitting, Guru handed her the shoe. Although Guru had worn it now many times, it was still shiny and bright. Guru always, always polished the shoe after one of their trips.

The mother looked at the shoe suspiciously. She turned it upside down and looked at its sole. It was ridged and black and shiny. In fact, she saw bits of her own face in the bottom of the shoe's sole. Then she examined the sides. Also shiny. Once again, she found her nose and her mouth—a bit distended—reflected in the side. The front of the shoe scared her. Although the shoe's features were ones that most people would've called attractive, Ma thought the shoe looked somewhat sly. Its eyes were small and beady and black. Its tongue was too long. It looked as if it would flick any minute and eat a passing fly. She handed the shoe back to Guru without saying a word.

Guru knew his mother would be furious if she knew of the trips he took with the shoe. So he just held the shoe and waited to be told what to do next. Nothing. His mother didn't say a word. She didn't ask him to leave, she didn't ask him to stay, and she didn't scold him. She just sat there lost in her own thoughts. Guru shifted from one foot to the other, a bit scared of her silence. Then his mother got up and started walking towards the kitchen and said as she was leaving, "Wait here, Guru." As soon as his mother was outside the room, Guru whispered to the shoe, "What's going on? What do I do?" and the shoe answered, "Just wait." Guru's mother came back carrying a large plastic Ziploc bag. She held her hand out to Guru for the shoe, and without a word he handed it to her. Then his mother said, "You may go to bed now, Guru." And Guru mumbled, "But what about my shoe? What are you going to do with my shoe?" His mother looked at him closely but didn't reply. Instead, she turned the shoe upside down and round and round. Then she poked its sides and pressed its nose hard. Guru squealed, "Ma, don't do that. You're hurting the shoe." And his usually loving Ma, who had become strange and cold, answered, "You can't hurt a shoe. Leather is not alive. Now go to bed, Guru," and she reached out and kissed him goodnight. "Remember to brush your teeth and wash your feet."

Guru turned away slowly and started climbing the stairs up to bed in a slight daze. He knew something awful was going to happen to his shoe, but he didn't know why. Why was his mother keeping the shoe? Was it the shoe's fault that the elf hadn't been in the market? Guru didn't think so. What was Ma going to do with the shoe? He'd have to creep back down later at night and rescue it, he thought, although, of course, his mother would know who was responsible. Maybe he should tell her of his excursions and that the shoe talked. But Guru didn't dare go downstairs again.

Slowly he changed into his pajamas, brushed his teeth, and washed his feet. That's when he really missed Shoe. Usually, when Guru had washed his feet, Shoe would say, "Nice and clean for me," and grin at him from the corner of the bathroom. Shoe didn't like getting wet, but he did like getting cleaned. After washing his feet, Guru would usually cream Shoe with a special white cream so the shoe could shine. After both were sparkling, Shoe and Guru, they would both get to bed for a few hours. Then at some point in the night Shoe would be near Guru's pillow, gently nudging him awake, and whispering, "C'mon, sleepyhead, let's go. There are places to be seen and things to be done. C'mon, c'mon, c'mon." Then Shoe would offer a few suggestions for that night's excursion, such as "Shall we go to the empty market by moonlight?" or "Shall we take a walk along the river?" or "Shall we zoom across one or two highways?" This last was always Shoe's favourite and the one Guru liked least, although he had to admit he too felt the thrill of danger that so excited Shoe. But on the whole, Guru preferred to choose the market by moonlight or the river in the dark. He always asked Shoe to take him to the elf, but the Shoe always refused.

Guru lay down for a while so that his mother would be fast asleep before he rescued Shoe. He couldn't sleep, of course, worried as he was. About two hours or so later, Guru crept down the stairs. When he reached the bottom, he stood quietly for a minute, wondering where his mother had kept the shoe. Suddenly he heard voices, and tippy-toeing along he followed them to the kitchen. What he saw in the dimly-lit kitchen was so shocking that he froze. In the ghostly light that came from the lamp on the kitchen table, Guru saw

a woman, a large woman wearing a flowing white robe. Her hair was loose and hanging down, and her arms were stretched out. In one hand she held his lovely red shoe. In the other, she had a small paring knife that she was dangling above the shoe. "I'll pinch your little eyes," she was saying, "before I gouge them out with this knife if you don't tell me about the wicked, weird, evil elf who made you. Don't think I don't know that something very strange is going on here. I'll pull your lovely, long, corrugated tongue before I slice it into ribbons. I'll spit on you and rub you in the kitchen trash so you'll have cucumber peels, mango peels, chicken bones and left-over *rajma* all over you. Then I'll put you back in this Ziploc bag, stomp on you, and either throw you out in the dumpster outside the city, or mail you to another town. Or bury you, or burn you. How's that, Shoe?" And with that she started pinching his eyes, first one little shiny black eye and then the next shiny black eye.

Guru was shocked. He had recognised the woman in white as his mother, but this mother he had never seen before. Her voice was strange and high. What she was saying and planning to do was mean and unlike herself. But she'd started doing the things she'd threatened, because the shoe suddenly went "Ouch" after the fifth pinch. "Ouch, ouch, ouch. Stop, you wicked woman. Why are you hurting me?" screamed the shoe as the knife came closer. Guru's mother looked triumphant as she said, "Well, so we talk, don't we? And we talk after only five pinches. Will one eye gouged out bring me the elf or shall I take out all ten? Or, shall I leave them un-gouged? Shall I leave you looking pretty, because you're a smarter shoe now than you were?" And Shoe answered immediately, "Oh, please, ma'am, please, I'll tell

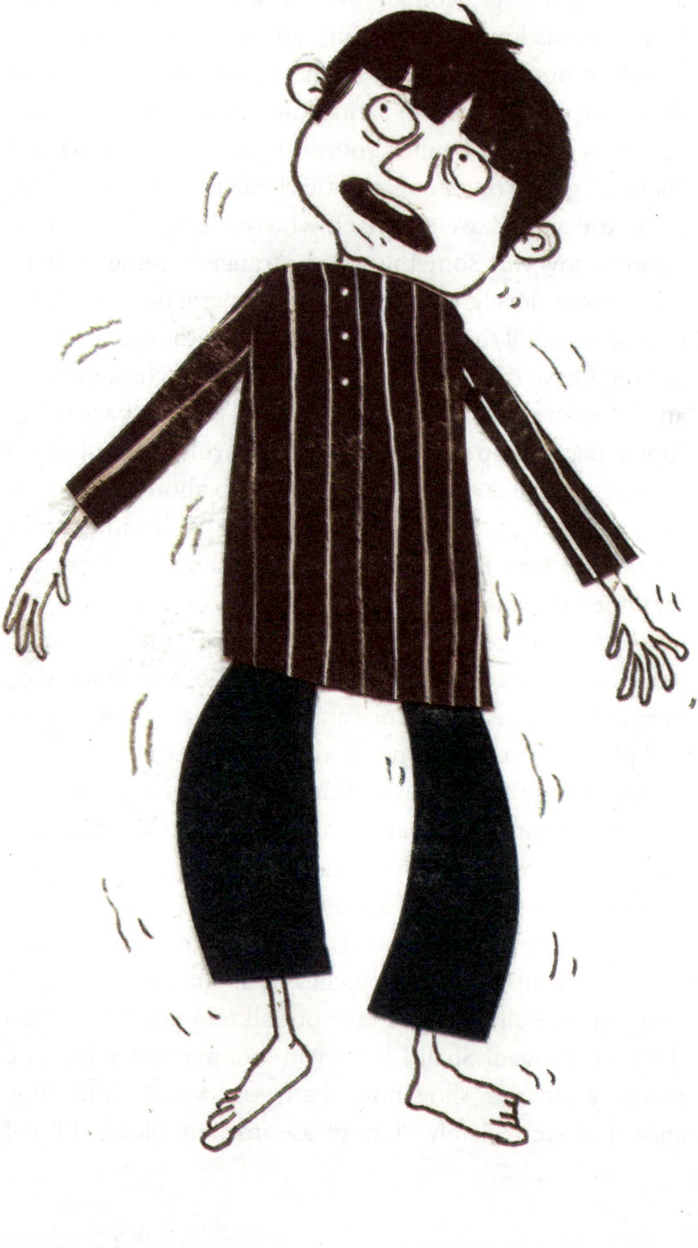

you all; I'll tell you all, but don't hurt me. I'm not wicked, nor is the elf, and please don't hurt me anymore." Slowly, from each eye a small tear came out and glistened on top of the red leather. Even Ma was struck by the tragic beauty of the crying shoe. So she said, "Okay, let's sit and talk," and turned towards the table to place the shoe on it. As she did so, she saw Guru standing outside the kitchen, looking terrified. Ma put the shoe down, stretched out her arms to Guru, and placed her scared son on her lap as she said, "Come, Guru, let's listen to Shoe." Guru crept into her arms gratefully because she had become a gentle-looking mother again as soon as she turned around and stopped torturing Shoe. The white lady, the woman with the terrifying voice and manners, had disappeared.

"Before you begin, Shoe," said Ma, "let's get one thing clear. I know Guru is involved in this. I know now that Guru was telling the truth about your doing what you wanted without his agreeing. But don't try to protect him. Remember how it feels to be pinched, especially the little teeny-tiny pinches? Well, there're lots more in my fingers. So tell the truth and trust me. I need to know what's going on and why. I need to know about the evil elf." Shoe looked extremely deflated as he looked at Ma and Guru. He was sitting on top of the Ziploc bag, on the table, but he looked like he had no life in him. Of course Ma had held him down by tying the end of the shoelace to the leg of the table. Clearly Ma knew just what Shoe could do and just what he hoped to do.

Shoe looked up sadly at Ma, and said, "An elf made me, it's true. He made many other shoes like me and many others not like me. But I don't know anything more about him. I just know he makes red shoes and lives in the woods with his son, the tyrant." "Why is his son the tyrant?" asked Ma. "Because he makes his father make only left shoes," answered Shoe. "And what does the son do?" Shoe told them he didn't do anything; he just wasted the money his father had saved years earlier. Although the son was a trained cobbler like his father, he refused to work. Instead, he made sure his father slaved away all day making left shoes that were never sold.

Shoe said that's why they couldn't find the elf in the market. After Guru had bought one left shoe, the son decided that his father would no longer go to the market. Now his father's life was even lonelier: he made shoes in the forest and nobody, nobody but Shoe brought him news of the outside world. Nobody stopped to talk to him except Shoe. He went there at night, three or four times a week. The market people were glad not to have an Irish elf in their midst any longer. They had never liked having this stranger there, anyway, especially once he started making only left shoes. Shoe started crying. Even Ma's eyes had a funny glitter to them. Before she could say it, both Shoe and Guru said, "We have to help the elf." All three agreed that must be done, but the question was how. "We'll all three think and then discuss in the morning," Ma said. "And Shoe, you're sleeping downstairs tonight." Saying that, she took Guru off to bed where she kissed him tenderly and whispered, "We'll make things alright, don't worry. And don't worry about Shoe either." Then she returned to the tied shoe waiting patiently on the table. "You sleep here tonight," she told him, "and we'll discuss our options in the morning."

Next morning, Ma and Pa were brightly waiting with Shoe at the kitchen table when a sleepy Guru stumbled downstairs. He hoped he could use Shoe to get to school today or he would really be late. Shoe wasn't at the table but was sitting on the floor next to the table. He was no longer tied to it, Guru noticed happily. "Good morning, Guru," said his mother brightly, all trace of the white witch from the night before having vanished. "Here, eat your cereal quickly or you'll be late for school. Shoe will take you there and tell you what a wonderful plan we have." Guru looked from his mother to his father, puzzled by their delighted faces. Shoe and he exchanged a quick glance, but after that Guru concentrated on finishing his cereal and hopping into his shoe. Bye, bye, bye, kiss, kiss, kiss, and off Guru went, hopping along in his shoe in a way he never thought he would again. Guru could hardly wait to hear what the plan was, but Shoe said he wouldn't speak until they were at the school, for Guru was so late.

Once they reached school, Guru sat outside and took Shoe off while Shoe filled him in on the plan. "Your parents are smart," he said, "they began at the end, not the beginning. They said, what would be the best thing that could happen to Elf? And they agreed, as did I, that the best thing would be for Elf and his son to live separately and for Elf to make pairs of shoes and not only left ones. So, this evening, when everyone gets home, we are going to decide how to do just that: to get Elf away from his son and allow him to make right shoes for all the left ones just sitting in the woods. You too should think about how we can do this."

Guru was excited all day creating plans for rescue. They could get a small army and fight the tyrant. They could steal Elf and his shoes away. They could go to the police. Maybe just Shoe and Guru could go and rescue the elf. When he shared these plans with Shoe on their way home, Shoe didn't say anything except, "Let's see what your parents have in mind. They're so smart."

When the whole family was gathered around the kitchen table, and Shoe was placed on a bag on the table, Pa said, "Well, Guru, you know what we need to achieve. But what is the best way to get to our goal? What plan should we pursue?" Guru was a bit tongue-tied at having to begin the discussion. What should he say? He somehow knew his father wouldn't like the idea of a little army of invaders. He also knew his father wouldn't like the idea of either a fight or theft. What would his father do if he were presenting his own plan? Guru thought quickly, but nothing was coming to mind except armies, theft, and the police. "Well, Guru," prodded his father and Guru said, "Well, Pa, why don't we go over and talk to Elf and his son?"

Guru was as shocked as all the others at the table by what had come out of his mouth. What a silly idea, he was thinking, what a stupid idea to talk to a tyrant, when he heard his father clap his hands and his mother give him a joyous smacking kiss as they both beamed at him happily. "Oh, Guru, I am so proud of you," said his father and mother together. "What a wonderful, mature idea. Let's talk to the elf and his son first, and see if that won't help matters," said his father. "Talking *always* helps," echoed his mother, looking fondly at her husband. "I know talking *always* helps." Shoe and Guru looked at each other slightly bewildered, but neither said a word. Instead, they went along with the family plan of talking to the elf on this coming Saturday, when everybody would be home early from work or school.

Guru was so excited he could hardly wait for Saturday. He was also terribly proud of himself because he had come up with an idea his parents really, really liked. They had told him he was so mature. His mother had confided that she had secretly feared Guru would want to take a little army over to Elf's house. She said she understood why he'd want to do that, but she was so proud of her young son who had grown up sooooo much in these past few weeks. After all, she said, it was a good thing he'd bought that shoe. Guru was suddenly so much more thoughtful and responsible, she said.

When Saturday came, a bright and cheerful Saturday, Guru leapt out of bed at the first sign of light. "Let's go and finish my half-day at school," he urged sleeping Shoe. "Let's go, let's go." Shoe was not in the same ebullient mood as Guru. Instead, he was withdrawn and silent and frowning. His nice round brow looked creased. His normally sprightly tongue looked slightly withered and sad as it drooped out of his mouth. Instead of his usually bright, shining eyes, he seemed to have dull, beady ones. Guru couldn't understand how the Shoe he had polished with extra care the night before could look so washed out, sad, and dull. "What's wrong, Shoe? What's wrong? Look, we're going to see Elf. We'll make him happy. His son will say okay, and everything will be fine." Shoe didn't seem to agree. He remained silent, lost in his own thoughts. When he hopped Guru to school, he did so tiredly, with no friendly chatter and no friendly invitations to visit strange, unknown places. Guru could tell he was worried, so after a while he too became quiet. But he remained excited. After all these months, he was going to see Elf again. He was going to go to some unknown parts of the woods. His mother and father would be with him, so he didn't even have to feel guilty or unsafe. Yes, Guru could hardly wait.

After lunch, by 3pm, the whole family was ready for their trip to meet Elf. Guru wanted to wear Shoe and everyone agreed that it was a fine idea. A strange crew made its way into the forest that afternoon. Ma, Pa and Guru were wearing shorts, t-shirts, and sneakers. Ma was carrying a small hamper of goodies in which she'd placed cookies, cake, and lemonade. Pa was carrying a walking stick that he didn't need, but that he liked very, very much. Guru was carrying one white sneaker and wearing, as usual, mismatched shoes. With his red shoe, Guru wore a white sock and with his white sneaker a red sock, a habit that was now almost as old as his meeting with Shoe.

Ma and Pa had not seen Shoe and Guru hopping for a long time, so the two put on quite a show. Shoe hopped

Guru far into the distance so that Ma and Pa worried they had disappeared. They were just about to panic when the two returned. Then Shoe decided to show off by turning quick pirouettes so that Guru was a small, circling blur as his parents got dizzy just looking at him. In this playful manner, Shoe led them through the outer trees of the forest to the inner trees of the forest where green, yellow and orange mushrooms grew and where sunlight only came through in small patches. Guru was now holding his mother's hand, he suddenly felt scared. Shoe, who had been showing off earlier, was now being walked along rather than doing the walking. The cookies and lemonade had been finished long ago.

This subdued group approached a little clearing in the woods where two small wooden houses stood. One had a padlock on the outside and from inside this house a steady hammering could be heard. The other house had its door wide open and the sound of heavy snoring came from within it. A modest wood fire burnt on one side of the clearing. On top of this fire, a round black pot was bubbling and the smell of freshly cooked rice pervaded the air. Opposite the fire was a tiny well, next to which lay a brass bucket on its side. "Tyrant is asleep," whispered Shoe, "and his father is working in the small hut there. Let's go say hi to him," and Shoe's face lit up at the prospect. "How?" asked Pa, "when the door is locked?" "Oh, the window," said Shoe, and asked Guru to take him off. As soon as he was off Guru's foot, Shoe leapt up to the narrow window ledge on the side of the hut. "Hi, Elf," he said in a cheerful voice, and there at the window Elf appeared. "Hullllo, Shoe," he said brightly and then suddenly went quiet when he saw Ma, Pa and Guru.

He looked at them for a long time without saying a word. Then with tears in his voice and eyes, he said, "You are the boy who bought the only shoe I have sold in a long time. You are the mother who helped me earn some money. I thank you," and he bowed his head. Ma's eyes were wet with tears; Guru was sobbing and snuffling into his hand. Pa was the only one looking composed. But now Elf had stopped crying and was looking very worried instead. "Why are you here?" he hissed. "Shoe, why have you brought them here? You know what my son will do. He'll be so, so angry. Quick, run away, before he sees you all. Quick, please go."

Shoe looked helplessly at Pa who said, "No, we have come to help you. We want to talk to your son." "But what will you say to him?" Elf asked. "He's a mean boy and he only wants to hurt me." Pa shook his head and said, "You don't worry. You go back to work. We'll sit and wait quietly for your son to get up. Please, we must do this. Just don't worry. Come, Shoe, come sit with us." With that, Pa led his little family to the bubbling pot on the stove. "Wife, isn't the rice burning?" he said. He was right. The rice was ready, but the cook was still fast asleep. There was nothing for it but to tend to the rice. So Ma took the pot off the fire using the red rag lying there. Then she saw that lots of fresh, green vegetables lay neatly chopped nearby. Might as well put them in, she thought. The tyrant must be making a *khichri*, since she couldn't see any other pots around. "What are you doing, Ma?" asked Guru in a worried voice. "Why are you cooking for the tyrant?" "I'm not cooking for the tyrant," answered Ma irritably. "I'm just using my time and making sure nothing gets spoilt. That's always a good thing to do."

Shoe was nodding along approvingly and saying, "Tyrant always boils everything together." Ma clearly didn't think much of that idea. She told Guru, "This hodge-podge is going to need some ginger. Go see if you can find any by the side of the house." Reluctantly, Guru went for a quick walk around the two huts. Indeed, his mother was right. Behind Elf's hut was a simple open shed under which lay carrots, potatoes, fresh turmeric and ginger. He picked up some of each and brought them to his mother who looked delighted. Like a little wizard, aided by Pa's Swiss army pocket-knife, she chopped the potato and carrot, and squashed the turmeric and ginger, and added everything to the pot along with fresh water that Pa had brought from the well. Elf was watching everything from the window, but he continued to hammer at a piece of leather so that his son wouldn't be woken up by the sudden silence.

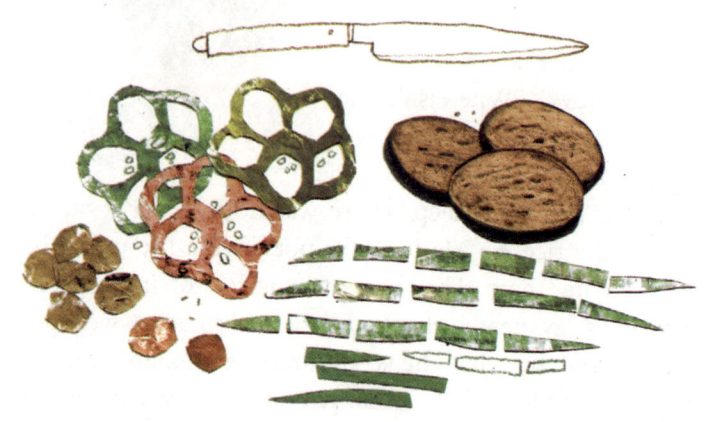

"Well, dinner is ready," announced Ma suddenly and everybody looked at her expectantly, with pleasure shining in their eyes. That khichri smelled so good. "Well, dinner is ready, but it's not our dinner," said Ma this time, so that Pa and Guru could remove the greedy look from their faces. "It is my dinner," said a voice behind them, to their shock. Everybody looked in the direction of the voice. Standing in the door of the second hut was a small, small elf. He was so tiny that he could've been missed as a blot in the shadow if he hadn't spoken. "I want my dinner," said the tiny tyrant elf, and he came across to the fire holding two tin plates. Ignoring everyone around him, he heaped spoonfuls of fresh khichri on the plates. One of these he placed on a flat stone nearby and then went and unlocked the padlock of his father's hut. Elf came out, picked up his plate from the stone, and just sat down to eat, ignoring all the people around him. His son did the same.

"This khichri is yummy," said the tyrant elf. "I've never had such a good khichri. Thanks, Lady. I suppose you cooked this?" Before Ma could answer, Elf said, "It's just like the khichri my wife used to make." He had tears in his eyes, and he brushed them away sadly. Ma didn't know what to say. Here was a sad father and his angry son, both enjoying her mishmash, hodge-podge khichri. So she said, "I'll make it for you again, whenever you like. In fact, why don't you come over some time and have dinner with us?" as if she were inviting her neighbours over for a homey meal. On hearing this invitation, Tyrant Elf suddenly woke up to the reality around him. In a gruff voice he asked, "Who are you? Why are you here? Why are you cooking my food? Why are you *eating* my food?" Indeed, Guru was eating, so ravenous was he after smelling the good khichri. He had heaped it into a tin cup and was shovelling it into his mouth as if he was starved. "Guru, what are you doing?" shrieked his mother in embarrassment. "I'm so hungry, Ma, and it smelled so good," Guru whined. To everyone's surprise, Tyrant Elf said, "I don't mind him eating. He's a small boy. He must be hungry, especially since his mother made the khichri. I never had a mother who cooked for me."

Tyrant Elf asked again, "Well, who are you all?" Nobody answered for a while. Then Ma said, "Well, it's not important who we are. What's important is that you're unhappy and your father is unhappy. So why don't you come and spend a few days with us? I'll cook you khichri and lots of other good things, and you'll also learn how to cook some of those things. Meanwhile, your father can make some different kinds of shoes for a change. You know, some right shoes? What do you think?" She asked the question not only of the two elves but of her husband as well, since this was a new plan nobody had discussed earlier. Pa was nodding fondly at his wife, and Guru was delighted at the prospect of two elves living in his house. Tyrant Elf, however, did not look delighted. He was scowling and suddenly stood up, letting his tin plate clatter off his lap. "Who are you? Why have you come here to cook me khichri and to invite my father and me into your house? Either answer me or get off my property, now."

Now Pa spoke softly and said, "Guru will tell you the whole story. Guru, could you please tell this young man why we are here? Start from the beginning and tell him everything, including your excellent idea of talking. Come, why don't you start." Guru swallowed and started speaking, even as his hand stretched out behind him to hold his shiny red shoe who had been hiding there the whole time. Guru quickly told all that had happened since he first went to the market with his mother and saw the red shoe. "Then one day," he said, "Ma and I went back to the market, but we could not find Elf. Nobody knew about him; nobody could tell us that he had ever been in the market. That's when my mother realised that there was something strange going on. After all, she had seen Elf and paid for the shoe. So, that night she asked Shoe to tell the truth, and Shoe told her about you and Elf, and how he can only make left shoes because you won't let him make others. And Shoe told us you hate your father because your mother died, but we know that he's a good elf and his wife died because she did. And then Ma and Pa asked me what we should do to help Elf and you, and I said we should come and talk to you instead of bringing a small army to rescue Elf. So, here we are." And Guru stopped, breathless with his performance, which he hoped was okay. He looked at Ma and Pa inquiringly, and they were both looking pleased. Elf had a funny, soft look on his face. Only Tyrant Elf looked distant and uncomfortable. Shoe was smiling at Guru, also happy with him. Everybody sat silent for a while, waiting for Tyrant Elf to speak.

The little elf didn't speak. He just looked from one to the other, and every time he looked at his father, he looked angry. But he didn't say a word. Instead, Elf spoke: "I'd like to go with this family," he said. "I'd like to go with this family for a few days while you think about what you want. You can come and see where they live, and that way you'll know where to find me if you want me back here." Tyrant Elf wasn't looking pleased with this idea, but he did seem puzzled about what to do. So Ma stepped in again and said, "Do you like freshly grilled quail with an onion and ginger *masala*?" Tyrant Elf found himself answering that he'd never eaten quail and asking what it was. "Well, I'll cook some for us tomorrow night, how's that?" Ma answered. "Now why don't we head home since we've all had an exhausting time? Elf, please pick up your tools and some leather. Come." Ma spoke so matter-of-factly and calmly and lovingly and warmly that nobody questioned her plan. She put her hand out to Tyrant Elf and said, "Let's lead the way." Tyrant Elf was surprised but allowed his hand to be held. Ma chatted the whole way, about her work, about the names of plants, about the hidden mushrooms beneath the leaves. Tyrant Elf didn't say much, but he walked along happily enough. Next came Pa and Elf. Pa was helping Elf carry some of his tools and kept asking him questions about different ones. Elf seemed delighted to talk about his tools and his shoes. Guru and Shoe were prancing around behind the whole group, thrilled with how the visit had gone.

When the group got home, Ma made everybody sit down at the table for a nice hot meal of green beans, *mutter aaloo*, and chicken kebabs. Tyrant Elf had never eaten such nice food in his life. When dinner was over, Ma suggested he stay for the night since it was such a long walk back. He agreed easily enough, but Ma made sure that he was in a separate room from his father. Elf got up to say a formal goodnight before everyone went to sleep. He thanked Ma and Pa, and then said, "Mostly, I thank your young son, Guru. I knew the day he bought a shoe that something would change. And now, thanks to him, I think there is some more change in the air. Change is wonderful," and he bowed again in his strange, formal way.

Elf got down to work in the garage the next day. The first thing he did was make a right shoe for Shoe. By that night, Guru was the proud owner of a beautiful pair of red shoes. He was thrilled, as was Elf, who had been singing all day long: "I'm making right shoes, I'm making right shoes." And Tyrant Elf? Well, Ma had untyrannised him, through food! After having eaten the special weekend family breakfast—blueberry pancakes—it was obvious that Tyrant Elf was putty in Ma's clever little cook hands. By the end of the day, he was helping her in the kitchen, ignoring his father, but not saying a word about going home either.

Only a few months later, Elf was a successful shoemaker who sold pairs of beautiful red, blue, green and black shoes. And Tyrant Elf, who everybody now called Elfy, had become quite a cook. Ma only helped him in the kitchen now, and she was encouraging him to join a chef's school. Nobody ever spoke of the clearing in the woods. Guru wore his matching red shoes with matching socks whenever he could. Although he was fondest of his left shoe, he was delighted to have two friendly, prancing shoes instead of one. Ma had new black shoes too, while Pa's new ones were brown and beige. Ma and Pa never asked Guru if he still went off to unknown places with his magic shoes, and Guru never brought up his secret adventures either.

Joey and his Mood

Joey and his mood got up together every morning. Some days when they got up, Joey's mood would say to him, "I'm sad today." Then Joey would try to think of why his mood could be sad. On other days, they got up very happy. On those days, Joey just jumped out of bed and got ready for school. He didn't have to find out why his mood was happy, although sometimes it would occur to him anyway. Then he would say, "Oh, I know, I'm so happy because I got an 'A' yesterday," or "Oh, I'm so happy because John E. is coming to play with me after school." Joey was always right. He knew his mood.

Finding out why his mood was sad could be hard. Sometimes it could take a whole day to find out. All day long, as Joey went to school and ate his meals and played with his friends and brushed his teeth and did his exercise (yes, Joey exercised every day, a few sit-ups and push-ups and some jogging), he would be trying to find out why his mood was sad. Was it the grey sky? Sometimes it was. Could it be that his mood was sad because his parents had a fight the night before? Yes, that always made it sad, even when they were not fighting about him or about anything important. Sometimes Joey never found out why his mood was sad. It just was. Joey hated those days. Even though he did everything the same as usual and even had fun, some little part of him was trying to get to know his mood and understand why it was sad.

But his mood could be quite tricky. It could run away with him and take him far away from where he was. Sometimes his mood would run him back into yesterday and then forward into tomorrow and even down into the dark of the night's dreams. On those days he would often go to bed upset. Then his mother would say, as she was tucking him in, "What's the matter, Joey? You've been sad all day. What's making you sad?" Joey, in a small voice, would answer, "I don't know, Ma." Sometimes his mother would make him talk about his day, and as he did, she would ask, "And did this upset you?" or "Did that upset you?" When she did this, she could sometimes find out what Joey had been trying to find out all day. Suddenly, when she said, "Was it this?" a light bulb would go off in Joey's head (just as in the comic books), and he would start smiling. It was *this* that had made him sad, but it had taken him all day and his mother's help to find out! But Joey would be happy then because just knowing why his mood was sad made him happy. He was always happiest when he knew why his mood was his mood, even if it had taken him a whole day to find out.

Joey's mood was most helpful when he got dressed every day. Somehow Joey would know that he needed to wear a yellow shirt with his blue jeans or that he needed to wear his black t-shirt with his black jeans. Joey's mother had let him choose his own clothes since he was two years old. Even then Joey knew what he wanted to wear. One day it was yellow and then it was green and often it was black. But sometimes all the clothes were wrong, and then Joey wished and wished he didn't have to think about his clothes like he didn't have to think about his hat. That's because Joey wore his hat every day. It was white and cotton and floppy, and Joey loved it. He could pull it down over his eyes, or push it back on his head and make it look as if it was dancing. Every day, as soon as Joey got out of bed and brushed his teeth and washed his face, his hat went on his head. Whether he was in a sad mood or a happy mood, the hat was on. He always put it on before he had finished dressing for school, so that he had to take it off and put it back on many times as he pulled on his vest or t-shirt or sweater. Joey never minded taking his hat on and off. He just wanted to get it on as soon as possible, and so he put it on after brushing his teeth and washing his face.

When Joey first started wearing his hat, which his mother had bought him one summer when he was four, both she and his dad kept telling him to take it off. "Get that silly hat off your head," said his dad to Joey. "Get that dirty hat off your head," said his mother to Joey. Joey pretended not to hear what they said. Instead, he poured some more cereal into his bowl and stared at the floating rice, imagining he was eating little worms. "Yum," he murmured as he spooned the crawling worms into his mouth, only to feel his head thwacked because his dad had leaned over, pulled off his hat, and smacked his head gently. Joey did not like this one bit. He wanted his hat back, and he wanted no thwacks on his head. But Joey knew that he should say nothing right then. So, he said nothing and waited until his dad and mom had left the table. Then he took his hat and put it in his backpack and put it on his head only when he was in the school bus. Nobody at school asked him to take off his hat, and so he didn't. He forgot all about it until he got home, and his mother said, "Joe—ey, take that silly hat off your head." "Ma, I like it," said Joey in a slightly whiney voice. His mother caught the note in his voice that warned her that he might slip into a sulky mood, and so she didn't say anything. She knew that Joey's moods could sometimes come and stay for even longer than a day. When Dad came home that night, he

and Ma whispered for a while at the front door. Joey was sure his dad would say, "Joey, take that silly hat off your head," but to his surprise his dad didn't. Joey sauntered through the evening in a good mood with a dancing hat pulled back on his head.

All this happened when Joey was four years old. Now he was seven, and the hat had become a part of him. He kept it on always and only changed it for a black one for two months in the winter. Joey never liked this change. The black hat was not as comfortable as the white one. It was harder and didn't look like it could dance as well as the white one, but even Joey thought the white one looked a bit sad in the weak winter sunshine. Joey was glad that he lived in New Delhi, a place where the sun shone and shone and shone most of the time. If he had lived in a cold place, like Pittsburgh, where Grandma and Grandpa lived, then he would've had to wear all kinds of different hats. In the winter, he'd have to wear woolly ones, and they would poke and pinch and wouldn't dance, Joey knew. So, he was happy to be in New Delhi in the sunshine of the American School where he studied.

Joey's mood agreed that the hat had to go on every day, and his mood agreed when the pale winter sunshine asked for a black hat instead of a white one. So imagine Joey's surprise when one day, as Joey was pulling on his white hat, his mood said, "You look silly in that hat." Joey was shocked. His mood had never spoken to him like that before. Yes, sometimes his mood made him change his clothes several times in the morning before it thought Joey looked okay. Yes, sometimes his mood could be quite trying as it said, "Try the yellow t-shirt," and then said, "No, try the green one. The yellow looks awful," even though just last week the yellow had looked lovely at John E.'s birthday party. Joey had learnt that it was best to do what his mood wanted; otherwise, he could end up wearing the yellow t-shirt and not feeling the slightest bit sunshiney, even though he looked bright and cheerful. So Joey was upset to hear his mood say, "You look silly." First, Joey wondered if he should wear the black hat instead. No, that wasn't it. It was October, the sun was still shining brightly, and black would definitely look silly. But what could Joey do? Here was his mood saying, "You look silly." Joey looked at himself and saw a small boy, in black Levi's jeans with a green t-shirt. His face had a nice round nose and slightly shiny cheeks which his mother loved to pinch. His hair? You couldn't say very much about his hair. It was there, and it peeped out here and there in brown wisps from beneath his hat. But really it looked like he didn't have hair and just had a hat. After all, he did have a hat on, didn't

he? And he had worn *this* hat. (Well, he knew his mother did buy him new ones when the old ones got too tight and too dirty.) But he had worn a hat that looked like this hat for three years, and he had never heard his mood call him silly before. Now here was a problem.

Joey tried to figure it out. Why did his mood think he looked silly? Joey could not find an answer. Nothing. So he went to school just as he was, but he asked his mother if he could please go shopping with her after school. Sometimes his mother would come and pick him up in the car after school. She would always buy him an ice cream (and John E. got one too if he was there), and then they would stand outside the car until he had finished eating. Then they would start driving home, but they would stop at Sarojini Nagar Market on the way back. Joey loved this market. The papayas were always large and yellow, the oranges round and orange, the mangoes green and yellow and red. People rushed about everywhere. Shopkeepers sat still, but their throats worked all the time as they called out the prices of their vegetables. Small boys and girls ran around offering to carry the fruits and vegetables on their heads in little cane baskets. All the boys and girls had little rolls of dirty cloth that they twined into coils and placed on their heads before balancing their baskets on top. Joey loved watching them do this. It always cheered him up to see the boys and girls with their coils on their heads. So, on the day that Joey's mood told him he looked silly, he asked his mother if he could go shopping with her after school. "Of course, my dear," she said, "of course, you can. In fact, I was planning to go shopping anyway." That helped Joey's mood just a little as he left for school.

All through the day he kept hearing his mood say, "You look silly, Joey, you look silly." Joey tried not to listen, but it was hard not to. He was feeling a little bit sad because of what his mood had said. But he would feel better after he met his mother, he knew. At 2:30pm, when the bell rang, Joey rushed to the front of the line so he could run out of school before all the other kids. His mother was waiting, and off they went to the ice-cream man. A mango bar is what Joey had, enjoying the slightly tart taste of the mango and the sweet, sweet vanilla taste inside the tartness. Then they got in the car and Mahinder, the driver, smiled at Joey and patted him on his hatted head. *"Kaisa hai, baba?"* he asked Joey, and Joey answered, *"Theek hun,"* in a slightly distracted voice since he wasn't really feeling okay. Joey never lied to Mahinder, but now his mother was there. Even though her Hindi was bad, she would sense that Joey was unhappy if he talked too much, so he didn't say much more. But he added, *"Baad mein bataunga,"* as the car sped off towards the market. "Ma, can I stay with Mahinder at the market?" asked Joey as they got there. "Well, I need Mahinder with me to bargain with the *sabzi wallahs*," she said. "Why can't we three be together?" "Oh okay, Ma. But then can Mahinder take me to the market after he takes you home?" Joey asked. "What do you want in the market, Joey?" asked his mother. "Tell me and I'll get it for you." "I don't know," answered Joey, and it was true that he didn't. He just wanted to be with Mahinder in the market for a little while.

When they got there, his mother said, "Let's finish the vegetable shopping first, and then Mahinder can take you with him while I go look at some cotton tablecloths. Okay?" Joey was thrilled. This was perfect. Now he would have a little time alone with Mahinder to ask him what he really needed to know, which was if his mood was right after all and did he look silly in his hat? After papayas and mangoes and salad leaf and eggplant and tomato and cucumber and green chillies and coriander had been piled on top of a little girl's head in her cane basket, Ma said, "Okay, Mahinder, now you take these vegetables to the car. Then you stay with Joey and do what he wants, but come to Sahgal Brothers in half an hour to get me. I'll be looking at some tablecloths." Ma patted Joey's hatted head and set off in an opposite direction to Mahinder and Joey.

Joey was jumping by Mahinder's side, trying to keep up with his long legs. "Mahinder, Mahinder, *mujhe kuch poochna hai*," he said. Mahinder answered, "I know, I know, you're dying to ask me something, but let's just finish with these vegetables, okay. Here we go," and he lifted the basket off the girl's head and started stacking all the vegetables in the trunk of the car. Mahinder was very careful with everything that he did. Now he placed the mangoes and papayas at the bottom of the net basket in the car but not at the very bottom where he had already put the onions

JOEY AND HIS MOOD   99

and potatoes. Next he placed the eggplants and then the cucumbers and then the tomatoes, and then the salad leaf. The coriander came on top as if there was a little green crown being placed on the vegetables. Looking pleased with himself, Mahinder tipped the little girl the money they had agreed on and then said to Joey, "Okay, now you speak. And where do you want to go that you want to be alone with me?"

Now that Joey had Mahinder's attention, he felt a bit silly. But he had to ask and so he did. "Mahinder, do I look silly in my hat?" came out in a small, hesitant voice. Mahinder looked at him carefully, and then he took Joey's chin in his hand. He lifted his face upwards and turned it to the left and then to the right and kept gazing at him closely. "Why are you asking, *baba*?" he said, instead of answering Joey's question. "You wear your hat every day. It's you. So why are you asking today if you look silly?" Joey didn't know how to answer, so he decided to be honest. "My mood said I look silly in my hat," he blurted out. Mahinder answered, "Then you must be in a bad mood." Joey was surprised to hear this. He only knew his mood to be happy or sad. What was a bad mood? Was he in a bad mood? "What's a bad mood?" he asked Mahinder. Again, Mahinder considered before answering. Then he said, "Your mood is bad when things that don't bother you start bothering you for no reason. You wear your hat every day. Why does it look silly today? Either it looks silly every day or you're in a bad mood." This was a bit complicated for Joey, and now he felt wobbly inside. He thought he must have looked silly in his hat every day. So he asked Mahinder, "Do I look silly every day?" and Mahinder said, "You do if you think you look silly. And you don't if you don't." "But do I look silly?" asked Joey, getting restless with Mahinder's answers. "Baba, do you like your hat?" asked Mahinder. "Yes," answered Joey, "I do." But Mahinder had heard the slight hesitation in his voice. Now Mahinder said, "Come, I'll take you to a special shop." Joey went along, troubled. He still didn't know if he looked silly or if he didn't, and he didn't know if he was in a bad mood or not. He knew he was neither happy nor sad, but he didn't think he was in a bad mood, either.

Before long, Mahinder and Joey were deep in the market where Joey had never been before. Here, they stopped in front of a small shop which had hundreds of different coloured cloths flowing down from the ceiling. The shopkeeper sat on a bed on which a clean, white sheet was spread. Mahinder spoke to him in rapid Hindi, of which Joey didn't understand a word. "*Topi utaaro,*" said the shopkeeper to Joey, who looked bewildered at the instruction to remove his hat. But he did and held it in his lap. The shopkeeper reached forward, holding a long yellow piece of cloth in his hand. He brought Joey's head forward and took the piece of cloth. In a minute he had wound it around Joey's head in a low turban. Solemnly, he handed Joey a mirror and said, "Do you like this?" Joey did. He loved the turban. It made him look so dashing and so handsome. "Can I buy it?" he asked Mahinder. "I have some pocket money that Ma owes me." Mahinder spoke to the shopkeeper and a quick transaction took place. Mahinder handed the shopkeeper some money. The shopkeeper tweaked the turban on Joey's head and took his hat away from him and put it in a fresh, green, plastic carry bag. Then Mahinder and Joey were off to meet Ma at Sahgal Brothers. "Do I look silly?" Joey asked Mahinder as he noticed everybody looking at him and smiling. And Mahinder answered, "You look like a little prince. You even look like an Indian prince."

Ma was shocked when she finally recognised Joey and Mahinder. She was standing at the door of the shop, gazing right at them, without recognising them. Joey saw his mother's eyes on his turban and even on his face, but no light of recognition flashed in them. She moved her eyes away, stopped vaguely in the direction of Mahinder, and then shifted her eyes in the distance again. By now, Joey had reached right up to her, so he tugged her skirt and said, "Look, Ma, look, I'm a prince in a turban." Ma was brushing him off, thinking that one of the beggars in the market was pulling on her skirt. But it wasn't. It was Joey in a yellow turban. Ma shrieked, "Jo-ey! Where have you been? Look at you!" Joey was happy to be looked at. He had seen his reflection in shop windows as Mahinder and he had walked down the streets, and he liked what he saw. What fun it was to look like a prince in a bright new turban! It was such fun that he bowed to his mother as a prince might do and took her hand and said, "Do you like it, Ma, or do I look silly as I do in the hat?" Only when he said the words did Joey realise that maybe he agreed with his mood, after all. Maybe he did look silly in his hat, and that's why his mood had told him he looked silly.

Joey's mother said, "Oh, you look like a handsome prince," and bent down to give Joey a tight hug. She looked up and smiled at Mahinder and asked him how much money she owed him for the turban. "Nothing," said Mahinder, "it's my present," and Joey beamed up happily at him in thanks. The three of them then made their way back to the car where the door was held open for little Prince Joey to get in.

That evening, Joey came for dinner in his lovely yellow turban. He was wearing a fresh *kurta pajama* as well, so he cut a very dashing figure indeed. Ma must have told Pa what was going on, because Pa also came to dinner in his Indian clothes. Even Ma had changed and she was in a sari. They had a lovely Indian feast that night, and everybody treated Joey as if he were the prince he looked like. That night when his mother tucked him into bed, Joey thanked her for the lovely day. Then he asked her, "Ma, what's a bad mood?" His mother thought for a while and then said, "Well, it's when nothing seems to go right. It's when something happens like it always did, but you don't feel good about it even though you always have before. It's when no matter what happens, you don't feel good anyway. Why, are you in a bad mood?" "No, I'm not," answered Joey, "although I think I was this morning when I woke up. Then Mahinder bought me the turban and then I was in a very happy mood." "Yes," his mother agreed; his mood had certainly livened up once he got the turban.

Joey slept happily that night and woke up in a very happy mood the next day. He jumped out of bed, brushed his teeth, washed his face, and then reached out to get his hat from where it always lay for the night—on the chair of his desk. His hat wasn't there. For a small second, Joey was worried. Where was his hat? Then he remembered it was in a clean, green, plastic sack and not on the chair. The sack was lying on Joey's chest of drawers. Slowly he went to it and took his hat out. He put it on his head, but his mood changed when he did. Then he took his hat off and put the turban on instead. Immediately, he felt bright and cheerful in his yellow turban. Joey thought about what to do. His white hat made him feel sad and dumpy. He didn't want to wear it. Instead, he wanted to be bright and cheerful, but he knew he couldn't go to school in a turban. So he and his mood decided that a red t-shirt would have to do the job. He pulled it over his head, and then he took his hat and put it on the chair. His turban he placed on the seat of the chair as well, next to the hat. They could both wait until he got home.

Ma and Pa seemed very cheerful when they saw him at breakfast that morning. Neither said a word about his hat, but his mother ruffled his head and his dad gave him a little thwack and ruffled his hair too. Then off Joey went to school, without a hat for the first time in three years. Everybody noticed, of course, and they all said, "Joey, where's your hat?" and Joey answered, "It's at home on the chair next to my turban." "Your turban?" they asked, especially John E., and Joey calmly answered, "Yes, my turban. Mahinder bought it in the market for me yesterday, and he said that I look like a prince in it. I wore it for dinner last night with my kurta pajama and Dad wore his kurta pajama and Ma wore her sari, and we ate butter chicken with *pulao*." His friends were looking at him in surprise, but Joey didn't care. He was in a good mood and he knew why. It was not only because he had a yellow turban that made him look like a prince but also because he had taken off his hat. Suddenly, for no reason Joey could understand, he felt happy and free without his hat on his head. Now, Joey decided he was going to wear a hat when he wanted, a yellow turban when he wanted, and who knows what other kinds of hats and turbans at other times, as he wanted.

Fair and Unfair

Fair and Unfair were at the market to buy some new shoes. Fair was wearing a green frock with a wide, black belt. Unfair was wearing an orange tunic beneath which she had a pale pink slip. When she walked, the slip peeped out and made the orange tunic look lighter and brighter against it. Fair's green frock was a lime green. It fit her tightly on top and then spread out in a nice, wide skirt beneath the belt. Although Fair and Unfair were dressed differently for the first time, both had their hair tied back in ponytails. Their black hair shone even more on the tops of their heads than it did in the swinging ponytails they had behind their heads. Their ponytails were held in place with black bows which sat neatly on top of the tails.

Neither one really liked having a ponytail, but today their mother had been in a rush and had made their hair in the quickest way possible. Fair was unused to her hair sitting tightly and swinging in the middle of the back of her head. She kept moving her head from side to side saying, "Oh, this is funny, I feel I have a tail." Unfair swung her own head in response and said, "You do have a tail." Unfair was not enjoying her ponytail, but she was not not enjoying it, either. She just didn't feel it like Fair did. Instead, her hands kept moving to her shoulders where she wanted pigtails to be. Often, when Unfair was walking along, she would hold her pigtails in her hands, one on each side and pull them or twist them or throw them behind her shoulders as her mood took her. She was missing her pigtails.

Fair and Unfair were identical twins. They were the same height and the same width and had the same hands and the same feet and the same little noses and ears. When they were first born, even their mother couldn't tell them apart. Even when they were bigger babies, she couldn't tell them apart, especially because she liked to dress them in the same clothes. As babies, both Fair and Unfair had worn soft, white, cotton frocks that showed thick cotton diapers hanging underneath. They seemed to cry at the same time and to need a change at the same time. They even wanted to be fed at the same time. When they were a little older, they wore little frocks with cross-stitch smocks that showed little houses and a garden, little squirrels and nuts, or a piggy or two. Their frocks were always well starched and clean, and they always had matching underwear with their frocks. On the underwear, the little garden would be cross-stitched without the house, or just the nuts would be patterned on one side. Their shoes were black and shiny, and their socks were always a bright white. Everybody always remarked on how nice the two little girls looked.

The two little girls did look nice. They enjoyed looking clean and shiny. They also enjoyed tricking people. Since nobody could tell them apart, Fair and Unfair played a lot of tricks on the people they met. They confused their grandmother when she tried to feed them, so she often didn't know if she had managed to feed both or just one. They would run in circles around her and refuse to sit properly at the table, so she would tiredly hold out a hand with food in it for whichever mouth it found. Sometimes, when one of them had done something naughty, like pinch a cousin, she would refuse to own up and point to the other saying, "She did it." They would both be laughing because they knew nobody could tell the difference between them. Their mother or grandmother or aunt, whoever had seen one of them doing the naughty thing, didn't know which one to punish and so punished both. They would be told they couldn't play or that they couldn't eat dessert or that they had to be quiet. Fair and Unfair never minded. The only thing they minded was to be separated. If they were separated, they both cried separately wherever they were until they were brought back together. Then they would become quiet and sit down in some corner. They didn't hug each other or kiss each other after they were brought back together. They just began to look happy and complete.

When Fair and Unfair grew up a little, they started looking a little different. Unfair was a little thinner than Fair and had slightly larger ears. Everybody was relieved to see the difference because now they could tell the twins apart more easily. Then everybody realised that they could only tell them apart if they were together. If they were apart, you still didn't know which one was Fair and which Unfair. Only if the other was standing right there, head to head and neck to neck, could you tell them apart. When Fair and Unfair realised that people could only tell them apart when they stood next to each other, the girls decided to keep wearing the same clothes always, so that they could confuse people as long as possible. They decided that even though they liked their hair to be different, they would wear the same style whenever they could. So Fair let her hair be in pigtails one day, and Unfair allowed hers to be in a braid the next.

On the day they went to the market in different clothes, they had had a difficult morning. Unfair had dropped a big glob of ketchup on her green frock when she ate her omelette at breakfast. Their mother was not pleased. She had been rushing all morning with her young son, Neither, trying to get all the children ready so they could go shopping and buy new shoes and new clothes. It was Diwali, and everybody needed a new set of clothes to welcome the new year. When Mother saw the ketchup, she groaned. Oh, no, she thought, now both the girls will have to be changed. Then she looked at Fair sitting and eating her fried egg neatly. Well, Mother thought, Fair doesn't need to be changed. So Mother decided that she would make only Unfair change her frock. She said, "Unfair, go and change your clothes right away."

Unfair got up and turned to Fair saying, "What do you want to change into?" when Mother said, "Fair doesn't have to change. She's fine. Off you go, Unfair. Since you were so messy at breakfast, this will be your punishment. You'll have to wear different clothes. Anyway, you girls are too old now to dress the same. You're almost seven." Both Fair and Unfair were heartbroken. How could they wear different clothes? They never had. Yet their mother looked determined as she scooped more soft-boiled egg into Neither's mouth. She wiped the spill under his bottom lip too hard in her hurry, so Neither was about to start crying when the soft egg in the spoon found its way back into his mouth and surprised away his beginning tears.

Unfair left the table quietly, looking down the whole time. Fair was quiet as well and stared for a long time at the remaining omelette congealing in Unfair's plate. Then in a small voice she said, "Why are you punishing me? I never dropped ketchup on my frock. It's not fair." She waited for an answer, but her mother was busy wiping Neither's mouth with a small, wet towel before stacking the empty plates on the table. So busy was she with her tasks that she didn't even hear what Fair had said. After a minute, Fair repeated her complaint in a thin voice. "It's not fair, Mama," she said. "Why am I being punished? I never spilled ketchup." "Oh, you're not on that still, are you?" groaned her mother. "Fair is neither here nor there. What's fair got to do with it? I just don't want to help two girls change instead of one, and I just don't want to wash the perfectly good frock you have on which is already crushed from your sitting on it at breakfast. Okay?" For Fair, this was not okay at all. All she could think of was that she was being punished. Now she would be wearing one frock, and Unfair would be wearing another, and everybody would know they were different. Especially when they went out, both Fair and Unfair liked to look exactly like the other, down to their expressions, so they could trick people. How were they going to do that looking completely different?

Now Unfair came back in her orange tunic and showed her back to her mother so she could button her up. "Very good," said her mother absently, still busy clearing the table. "Are we ready then?" The girls nodded and left for the car, holding hands. Mother came carrying Neither in her arms. Then they all drove to the market in silence. The market was lit up with strings of white light and coloured streamers everywhere. Shopkeepers and the boys who helped them were outside the shops, trying to draw in new shoppers with their calls of bargain offers. Mother parked the car and started walking towards the shoe shop, past the men selling clothes that lay in heaps. One by one, as if they had agreed before, the shopkeepers held up cotton shirts and pants and called out, *"Sau rupaiye ka, Munni ke liye. Sau rupaiye ka, Babbloo ke liye. Sau rupaiye ka, Tinku ke liye,"* and even Mother was tempted for a minute to buy the shirts for unknown Babbloos, Tinkus and Munnis since they were just hundred rupees each.

Attracted by the lively sounds, Neither had turned his head to one side as the family walked straight past the clothes stalls. Mother was pushing Neither's stroller and holding Fair's hand, who was holding Unfair's hand. Sometimes to

FAIR AND UNFAIR   113

get through the press of people, the family would walk one behind the other instead of abreast, but they never let go of each other. Then as they reached the corner where the row of shoe shops started, Mother met an old friend of hers. The two women started chatting while the girls fidgeted and ignored Neither squirming in his stroller. Mother saw Fair and Unfair rubbing their shoes in the dust, and seeing they were restless suggested they walk down to the shoe shop, which was just three shops down the street. Pleased and still holding hands, the two girls skipped off while their mother watched carefully until they were at the store. That's when

Fair started swinging her ponytail and asked Unfair how she liked hers.

Fair and Unfair got to the shoe store and went in. The shopkeeper knew them. They had been buying their shoes here for years, ever since they were two years old and first started wearing shoes. "Hello, little girls," he said, "and are you out shopping alone today?" He smiled brightly at them, pleased with his own joke and happy to see them in the store. Fair decided to lie and said with a straight face, "Yes, we're shopping alone," just as Unfair said, "No, our mother is just behind us. She met someone in the market." The shopkeeper looked at them and started laughing. "So, one of you is making fun of me with a lie, and the other one is telling the truth. I know which of you lied. The green one. You must be Unfair."

Fair and Unfair looked at each other. They didn't say a word. They just stared at the shopkeeper, who was smiling at them. He began to feel a little strange, to have two little girls in their starched frocks, with their shiny hair, in their shiny shoes, holding hands and staring at him. Then he tried again and said, "Well, which of you is Fair and which is Unfair? And why are you dressed differently today?" Fair and Unfair both pointed at each other and said, "She wore a different frock." They had not planned to say this. But it had come out, at just the same time and in just the same way from both their mouths. Things like this happened to Fair and Unfair all the time, so they weren't surprised. But the shopkeeper felt uncomfortable and started looking outside his shop to see if he could spot their mother.

Luckily he could. She was just coming up to the store, smiling at him, as she pushed Neither along. The shopkeeper cooed at Neither, "Are we ready for shoes yet?" as the mother shook her head no. "I need shoes for the little girls," she said. "They're growing fast now. In a week, their shoes won't fit them. They're already too tight. And it's Diwali. They need new shoes and new clothes. Come on, girls, take off your shoes so he can see what size you need." Two pairs of black shoes were dutifully taken off. Two pairs of feet in bright white socks stood next to each other in the store. The shopkeeper made the girls sit down and put one foot each on a metal stand with numbers on it. "My, their feet have grown," he said, "but they are the same size. Exactly the same size. Well, do you want the same style of shoe?" Both girls nodded yes, and their mother nodded yes. Then the shopkeeper clapped his hands into the ceiling and yelled out something. Part of it was a number, and the other part was some sort of a secret code.

In a minute, two hands holding boxes of shoes appeared in a hole in the ceiling. Behind the hands was a head and part of a crouching body. The head yelled something short and dropped down the first box of shoes. The shopkeeper caught the shoes along the smooth length of the box. Then he flicked his hand, straightened the box, and laid it on the shelf above the metal stand in front of Fair. Then he turned back to look at the ceiling, held his hands up, and another box landed in his hands. Again he flicked the box straight and placed it on the metal stand in front of Unfair. Then he did the same thing twice again until there were two pairs of shoes in front of each girl. The girls just sat there with their feet held out in front of them, against the cool metal of the stand. The shopkeeper lifted their feet, one by one, and buckled their shoes on for them. One pair of shoes fit them perfectly. But Mother was fussing with these shoes and said, "These you'll outgrow in a month. I think you better take the next size." The shopkeeper was nodding in agreement. He pressed a finger on the tip of Fair's shoe and said, "There's no space to grow. The shoe is too snug." Without bothering to press Unfair's foot, he unbuckled both girls' shoes and made them wear the other shoes the man had thrown down from the ceiling. These were too big, but the shopkeeper said he could give them an insole. The shopkeeper always gave them an insole. He called something out to his helper who came with two pairs of insoles, which he tucked into the new shoes. Then Mother said the girls needn't wear their new shoes home. She said they could walk out in their old shoes. "No, Mama, I want to wear my new shoes," wailed both the girls. "It's not fair," they cried. "Why can't we wear our new shoes?" "Because they'll get scruffy in this market," said their mother tiredly. "Isn't that so?" she asked the shopkeeper, who was nodding in agreement. "Yes, they'll get scruffy," he said dutifully, and both the girls stared at him with an unfriendly look in their eyes.

"Madam," said the shopkeeper, "which of these little girls is Fair and which is Unfair?" Their mother looked at them, but the two girls had left each other's hands as they heard this question, and they had walked to different ends of the store. Both had their backs to their mother. Fair's ponytail was swinging from one side to the other, while Unfair held her head still. From the back, Mother couldn't tell which one was

Fair and which Unfair. Their ears looked the same, and they seemed exactly the same size. Mother couldn't remember which one had dropped ketchup on her dress that morning. Was it Fair or Unfair? Then she couldn't remember which one was wearing a green frock and which one the orange one. Then she wondered if it mattered and said as she paid the shopkeeper, "I don't know which one is which. One's Fair and the other's Unfair, but they look the same." Then she called to the girls, "Come on, girls, pick up your shoes and let's go finish our shopping," as she pushed Neither out of the store, followed by the girls. The shopkeeper stood at the door of his shop and waved to the family as it left.

While Mother pushed Neither along, both Fair and Unfair were swinging their new bags of shoes and holding hands. Neither was looking around from side to side at the lights and colors in the market. Mother turned around and said, "Girls, now when we go to buy new frocks, I want you to choose different ones. It's time you wore different clothes and started being two separate young girls. Okay?" Fair and Unfair looked at her and stopped walking at the same moment. They hadn't planned to, but they had just done the same thing. Mother had already turned around and was walking ahead, weaving Neither between the shoppers. Neither turned his head around completely in his stroller, staring at his two sisters standing in the middle of the crowd of shoppers. Their faces looked the same. Their arms looked the same, with a bag of shoes hanging on the outer side of each body. Except for the frocks they were wearing, they looked the same. Since Mother had still not noticed that the girls weren't coming along, Neither let out a loud cry. Then Mother also turned her head and saw her twin daughters staring at her. "Come on," she called. "Why are you dawdling?" Then she realised that the twins weren't dawdling. They had taken a stand. They were refusing to move.

Mother turned Neither's stroller around and walked back to the girls. She was angry. "Why are you wasting time?" she scolded them. "We have a lot of shopping to finish. We have to buy your frocks, new clothes for Neither, and *diyas* for the house. Why are you standing here in the middle of the road?" The girls didn't answer. Tiredly Mother said, "You need to start wearing different clothes. You are not children anymore." Both girls said, "Why? We want to wear the same clothes. It's not fair that we can't do what we want to do." Mother tiredly gave in and said, "Okay, okay. Buy what you want. Let's just go."

This time Mother made sure the girls walked ahead of her. Neither was looking happy now, and his head was facing straight ahead. When the family got to the clothes shop, Mother asked the shop lady to show some nice frocks in pink and green and blue. The girls liked the blue one best. It had a smock and a nice pleated skirt beneath. They already had blue bows they could wear with these frocks. Fair tried on the frock and it fit perfectly. The girls were looking happy with the blue frock. Then Mother tried again to get them to change their minds and said, "The green one is very nice, too. It's as nice as the blue one. Shall we take a blue one and a green one, girls, and you can see how you enjoy dressing differently? Aren't you enjoying wearing different frocks today?"

The girls were not enjoying wearing different frocks. Although they had noticed people looking at them twice as they always did, people were not looking at them as long and as hard as they did when they were dressed just the same.

So they both shook their heads and said, "No, we both want to wear the blue frocks." Mother gave in and nodded to the shopkeeper to do as the girls said. Then she said, "Now let's buy something nice and different for Neither. What does Neither want to wear?" Neither was sitting comfortably in his stroller, looking up at his mother. He did not look as if he was part of the same family. His face was a perfect round. On the back of his head was a perfect little circle from which his hair started rounding out around the round of his face. His eyes were ivory black and deep. They were also round, as was his nose and his chin. Even his slightly chapped rosy cheeks were round and plump. His voice was deep, surprisingly deep for a two-year-old, as if it had been aged with years of smoking and single malt whiskey.

"I want an orange shirt," he said, "and I want new black pants." It was the first time Neither had spoken so firmly about the clothes he wanted. Mother was surprised, as were Fair and Unfair. But Mother nodded to the shopkeeper who brought just what Neither wanted. His clothes were chosen in a minute. "Well, that was easy," said Mother to the shopkeeper when Fair and Unfair said, "Mama, we've changed our minds. Can we also have orange shirts and black pants?" Mother looked upset and said, "Why? Your blue frocks are so pretty." Neither was beaming at the girls with a knowing look in his eye. He cracked a slow smile. The girls insisted, "Please, Mama, please, please, we also want to wear orange shirts and black pants. Please." "Nonsense," said Mother firmly. "These clothes are for Diwali. You have to look nice on Diwali. You can't dress in any old thing, wear scruffy clothes and look like little boys." She turned to the shopkeeper to tell him to pack the blue frocks for the girls and the orange shirt and pants for Neither when the girls spoke again, quietly. "We don't want new frocks, Mama; we want new shirts and pants." The shopkeeper also chimed in and said, "They'll look so nice in these bright shirts and pants." Because it was Diwali and the start of the new year and because she was tired, Mother gave in and asked the shopkeeper to bring what the girls wanted.

"We'll all look the same at Diwali," said Neither, bursting with pride, as the family walked towards the shop selling clay diyas in packs of fifty and a hundred, all tied together with a rough string. Mother bought a hundred diyas, and the girls said they would ring the roof with lights the next week for Diwali. Then she looked at her three children and said, "I hope all three of you won't always want to dress alike," but none of the three children answered. Fair, Unfair, and Neither just looked at each other and smiled.

Soman and the Toot

In Cochin, there was a little scooter that was different from all the others. First, its name was Scootie. Although many other scooters were also called scootie, especially by tourists who came from Delhi, this one's *real* name was Scootie. Second, its back was wider than the backs of all the other scooters, including that of his cousin, Tony. This meant that much more sky came flooding into Scootie from behind than in all the other scooters that whizzed, sputtered, and tooted along the streets. When Scootie was empty, *all* the sky flooded in, whether it was grey or blue. Because of Scootie's special back, you could tell from afar if only one person was sitting inside or two, and you could tell if a whole family had squeezed in. When a whole family sat in Scootie, the baby's head would be higher than all the others, and the sky would have to fit in between the mother and the father and the older sister and the bags that the family was carrying.

Scootie belonged to Soman, a skinny, small guy with a lovely smile and yellowish eyes. He was a kind man, a man who drank only one glass of toddy every evening and that too with his wife as the family ate the fresh fish Soman brought home. When Soman came home on Scootie after a day of taking tourists from the old synagogue in Jew Town to the Chinese fishing nets, his wife would greet him with a smile and take the fish from his hands. Then she would wash the fish, rub spices into it, and leave it aside as she put out clean clothes for Soman to wear after his bath. Their five-year-old son, Dilip, would hang around Soman as he cleaned and polished Scootie before going in for a bath himself. Never did Soman allow Scootie to spend the night dusty and dirty. No, Scootie was always made as clean as Soman himself with fresh water and a good polish done with a clean, soft cotton cloth. Soman was especially careful to shine the frill around Scootie's back, which was a cheerful yellow, edged with green. On the frill, Soman had stapled small red squares. By the time the family sat down for a dinner of fried fish, vegetables and rice at the small table under the coconut trees, the red squares were so clean they looked like dancing stars.

One lovely moonlit evening, as Soman and his wife Lalitha sat talking under the trees, they heard a little tooting sound from the other side of the house where there was a small road on which sometimes other scooters and cars ran. First, they ignored the sound and continued sucking on the bones of the fried *meen*. Lalitha even cracked the bones between her teeth, chewing them in pleasure. The spices had seeped into the bones of the delicate fish and the crunching of spiced bones made her happy. Soman was listening thoughtfully to Lalitha's soft crunching when that tooting sound came again. After the third time, he said to Lalitha, "Should we go and see what it is? Maybe somebody wants us?" Lalitha started sucking the head of the meen and said reasonably, "If somebody wants us, why don't they come and get us?" "I don't know," answered Soman, "but I'm going to see who is tooting away into the peace of the moonlight." Soman put down his glass of freshly tapped toddy next to Lalitha's and started walking to the other side of the house. "I'm coming too, I'm coming too," said Dilip jumping up, happy to leave his fish and spinach on his plate. "No," said Soman firmly, "you're staying right here with your mother. You haven't finished your fish yet." Dilip sat down quickly, knowing he wouldn't be allowed to leave his dinner until he had finished it.

Now there was no interruption to the tooting. "Toot, toot, toot, toot," came the sound again and again and again as Soman disappeared around the side of the house. "Ma, this fish is smelly," said Dilip "and my stomach hurts." "Finish your food," replied Lalitha firmly and started pulling fish off the bones and feeding Dilip. He ate rapidly. "Toot, toot, toot," continued the sound as Dilip swallowed faster and faster. Mouth wide open, Dilip was waiting for the next mouthful, but his mother's hand had slowed down. The tooting sound had stopped. Everything was quiet and still under the moonlight. Lalitha put down what was left of the cleaned bones of the fish and said, "Let's join your father and see what's going on." Dilip quickly helped his mother pick up the plates so that the hungry cats hanging just outside the family circle wouldn't come and finish what was left of the fish.

When Dilip and Lalitha got to the other side of the house, they had a surprise. They looked to the left, all the way down the road that went on and on into the moonlit dark. They looked to the right, all the way down the road that went on and on into the moonlit dark. There was nothing to be seen. The sound of the sea came steadily from in front of them. Whoosh, went the waves, whoosh, whoosh, whoosh—always the same amount of time between the whooshes. But where was Soman, and where was the tooting sound? Besides the sea, there was nothing to be heard. Instinctively, Dilip had put his hand in his mother's. She was holding him tightly as she gazed down the left of the road and down the right of the road. Nothing. Look as they did, neither Lalitha nor Dilip could see or hear anything but the sea. "Soman," she called, "Soman, where are you?" But her words just got mixed up with the sound of the waves and disappeared into the dark. No sound of her husband's cheerful voice came back to her saying, "Here I am, Lalitha."

After looking up and down the road again and again, she said, "I think we should go inside." No sooner had she said the words than Dilip started pulling her towards the house. Once inside, Dilip didn't cling to Lalitha's hand as tightly as he had been doing outside. Lalitha too felt better than she had felt on the other side of the house. But she didn't know what to do. Where was Soman? And what had happened to that tooting sound? Dilip was looking up at her with big, frightened eyes. "What do we do, Ma? What do we do?" he kept asking, while pulling at her sari. "Where's Pa gone? Why has the sound taken him away?" "I don't know what to do," said Lalitha, trying to hide the fear she felt, the same fear she saw on Dilip's face. "I don't know," she repeated firmly. "What can we do? Your father goes to see what the tooting is, and he disappears into the dark along with the sound. What can we do? Nothing. It's time for bed." With that, she briskly led Dilip out to the back of the house so she could wash his face and feet before putting him to bed.

Out in the moonlight at the back of the house, everything looked peaceful. The coconut trees bent with their usual grace and let the moon come in latticed through their leaves. The table at which the family had had dinner was under the trees. The cats had already left since there was no food to be had. Scootie was shining in the white pale moonlight, with stars still dancing on him. Lalitha turned open the tap outside and started washing Dilip's face. He squished up his eyes and tried to get away from her rough hand, but she held him tight with one hand while using the other to briskly rub his face clean. "Ma, Ma," Dilip was trying to say past the water on his face and past his mother's hand on his face, "Ma, listen to me," he managed as he twisted his face away. "Ma, why can't we take Scootie and go look for Pa?" Lalitha heard this and immediately stopped rubbing Dilip's face. She hadn't thought that they could go looking for Soman in Scootie and slowly considered the idea. It was a good one. It was less scary than walking out into the dark. At least in Scootie they could go somewhere and go somewhere fast. "Let's go, Dilip," she said briskly.

Scootie was surprised to have Lalitha and Dilip sit on his front seat. He was used to Soman, who perched on half his bottom, somehow holding the other half in the air. Lalitha, on the other hand, sat firmly and fully on Scootie's seat. Scootie didn't mind, but it did feel strange. Dilip sat right next to her, his little behind making no dent in Scootie's seat. Lalitha had no problem starting Scootie. She knew just what to do, how to turn the handle to rev him up, and how to get going so that she and Dilip were around the house in a jiffy. When they were on the other side of the house, she slowed down and asked Dilip, "Which way?" as if he would know. Dilip pretended he did and said, "That way," pointing to the left. Off Lalitha went, driving on the dark road to the left of the house. The sound of the sea kept whooshing from the right of Scootie. The moon gave its white light to the road, but there was nothing to see except the moonlight. Lalitha drove so fast that Dilip had to hold on to her so he wouldn't fall off. "Ma, slow down," he said. "If you go so fast, we won't even see Pa if he's on the road." So she slowed down, and together they looked for some sign of Soman.

There was no sign. Dilip and Lalitha peered into the grove of coconuts where Eapen's house stood. It was all dark. Then they peered into Lalitha's mother's house near the lagoon. It was all dark. On and on they drove, Lalitha and Dilip, without any sign of Soman. No car or scootie came down the road. No person came down the road. And no sound came down the road. They could make out the school as they drove by it and the temple when they left it behind. On they drove down the lonely road in the thick moonlight to the whooshing of the sea, but there was no other sound, and there was no sight of Soman.

Suddenly Lalitha said, "I wonder if we should keep doing this. I don't know if there's any petrol in Scootie, and we have to get back," and she slowed down by the side of the road so she could turn around. As she did so, they saw the outside of an old church, crumbling and ghostly, in the moonlight. A stray dog was beginning to yap up to Scootie and was making small, barking sounds. Dilip was scared and tucked his feet up under him saying, "Hurry up, Ma, this dog will bite us." Ma did. She didn't like the sound of the dog either. She revved Scootie up so they could zip off, just as the dog barked louder and started sniffing at her feet. But as Scootie left the church, both Lalitha and Dilip heard a sound. "Toot." There it was. That was the sound that had taken Soman away. "Toot, toot, toot," came the sound suddenly again and again, even though Lalitha and Dilip were still driving away. "It's the sound, Ma, it's the sound," said Dilip, pulling at her sari. "Stop, it's the sound." Ma started slowing down, but she was afraid to stop. The dog was still barking, and Lalitha knew that if she turned around and went back, he would soon be yapping at her feet once more. But she slowed down and then finally stopped right where she was. The church was now in the distance. The barking came faintly from the church, and mixed into the barking came the tooting sound.

Lalitha and Dilip sat in Scootie for a few minutes, listening to the barking of the dog, the whooshing of the sea, and the strange tooting sound that came again and again. "What is that sound, anyway?" she said in exasperation. "I wonder what it can be? I think I've heard it before," she added half to herself. Then she shook her head and decided, "Let's call for your father. We can't get closer to the sound and go back to that dog." "Soman," she called as Dilip piped out "Papa." They both stopped almost immediately. "It's better if we say the same thing," Lalitha said. "Let's both say Soman." Then she added, as if to herself, "I can't call out Papa." Dilip had never used his father's real name before and felt very strange saying "Soman" there in the moonlit dark near the old church. But he did anyway, hoping his voice would help make his mother's louder and bring his father back from the tooting sound that had taken him away. "Soman, Soman," they called out, softly at first, and then louder and louder. But they needn't have bothered. No voice answered them. The barking of the dog got louder and the tooting sounded fainter as the dog started running closer and closer to Scootie.

"Quick, we better run and hide in the back," said Lalitha, jumping off the driver's seat dragging Dilip with her. Once in the back seat, she quickly dropped the tarpaulin that made for doors on either side of Scootie. This tarp kept the curtains of Kerala rain that fell for days and days out of the laps and shoes of the passengers. Once they had buttoned the tarp, both of them felt quite safe. Holding Dilip tightly, Lalitha leaned back against Scootie, just as the yapping dog reached them. He leapt on the sides, and they felt his weight through the tarp. Lalitha put up her feet, Dilip clasped tight in her embrace, and moved herself to the centre of the seat. Now even if the dog yapped all the way around Scootie, he couldn't reach them.

After a while, the dog grew tired. He had jumped and yapped and yelped and flung himself against the scooter, but there was nothing fresh to bite and nothing new to chew. Even licking Scootie's well-polished exterior wasn't rewarding. But the dog wasn't going to go away quietly. Oh no. He hadn't tired himself in the moonlight near a church to turn around and walk away. So he settled down by the side of Scootie and gave occasional barks to announce he was right there. Lalitha and Dilip breathed a little easier, but now they were totally stuck. Any movement and the dog would bark louder and more ferociously. "We might as well sleep," Lalitha murmured to Dilip, trying to rock him and herself to sleep. Slowly they both started relaxing to the sounds of the occasionally barking dog and the repeated toots. For the toots hadn't stopped. Through all of the events of the last minutes, the sound of tooting had continued, although soft and distant. "Ma, I wish the toot would come to us since we can't go to it," said Dilip in a pleading voice. "Yes," murmured his mother, just to soothe him to sleep. "Yes, perhaps your wish will come true, and the toot will come to us and bring your father along with it," she murmured, as she nodded off to sleep.

Just as they were drifting off, the sound of some voices mingled with the tooting. As the voices kept talking, they seemed to get louder and coming closer. Suddenly, Lalitha realised that the tooting sound was also getting louder. The voices sounded familiar. I know that toot, she thought, even as she huddled closer to Dilip, afraid of what the voices might bring. "I hope nobody stops near us," she was muttering to herself when the dog gave a nice loud bark. The voices seemed nearby, and the tooting was as loud as she had heard that whole evening. The dog was now barking steadily. Lalitha stayed huddled in her seat, still clutching Dilip. Then the sounds receded. A scootie seemed to drive away, and the tooting disappeared with it. In a few moments all was quiet again except for the sound of the dog. His barking became distant, and Lalitha realised that he'd been running after the voices and the tooting. "Maybe the tooting will take him away as well," she hoped, still trying to imagine and understand what she had heard.

Lalitha spent a lonely, lonely night holding Dilip in her arms. No voices or tooting disturbed them again that night. Only the sea crashed its waves and the moon rose higher. As the world became brighter in the moonlight, Lalitha felt frightened. She thought she saw strange shapes move in the distance, shapes that were coming closer. Dilip, who had been almost asleep when the dog began chasing the tooting sound, was also wide awake. "Ma, what is that monster?" he asked as they saw leaves of bushes move in the darkness. "Ma, what is that moving behind the church?" he asked moments later, sure he had seen something. Lalitha calmly kept saying, "It's nothing, Dilip, it's nothing," but she was scared too. Only holding Dilip seemed to help as they waited for morning to come.

As soon as there was enough light, Lalitha started moving around in the back seat. Every time she did, the dog barked. She was sobbing softly to herself in fear. She peered out the front of Scootie and said loudly, "Shoo." The dog yapped back. She tried again, more fiercely this time. Again the dog yapped. Then suddenly he squealed in pain and went limping off. She heard footsteps approaching and shrank back into the seat with Dilip. Then a man's deep voice said, "Lalitha? Are you there?" Lalitha couldn't recognise the voice, so she didn't answer. Again the voice said, "Are you there?" and now a hand moved away the tarpaulin from one side. Lalitha looked out hesitantly and saw her husband's brother Eapen standing there. "Eapen," she said in relief, "it's you. Do you know where Soman is?" Eapen looked at her strangely and said, "No, do you? I came to your house in the morning so Soman and I could go to Jew Town together, but there was no one there. No one slept the night in your beds. What's going on?"

Sobbing loudly, Lalitha said, "Soman went away. A sound took Soman away last night. We came looking for him, but we couldn't find him, and then this dog trapped us here. I don't know where Soman is." Eapen kept looking at her but didn't say anything. Then he said, "We should get home, no?" Lalitha agreed and said, "You drive Scootie." Leaving his own scootie, Tony, there near the ruined church, Eapen drove Lalitha and Dilip back in silence. When they got home, everything looked as it always did in the early morning sunshine. The birds were twittering, a few cats had moved up close to the back of the house, and a tap of water was running freely in the bathroom. Lalitha went from room to room calling for Soman. No one answered. Eapen had gone to fetch her mother who now arrived looking very worried. She came and held Lalitha and stroked Dilip and made both of them lie down as she made some tea. The rest of the day, friends and relatives kept dropping in to check on Lalitha and Dilip. She heard them whispering, "Poor thing, she's lost her mind. Thinks her husband ran away with a sound. Nobody runs away with a sound. He's obviously run away with another woman. Must be that new girl, Baby, whose father just moved here from Palakkad. Pretty thing she is. But she's not a good girl, running away with other people's husbands. And Lalitha so young also. So sad."

Lalitha tried not to listen to these voices, but it was hard not to. She asked Dilip if he remembered the tooting that took away his father. Dilip said he did. But when Eapen asked what the tooting sound could've been, both Lalitha and Dilip couldn't say. They couldn't describe it properly. "It was low," said Lalitha just as Dilip said, "It was a pointy, thin sound." Then Eapen asked, "Was it a human sound?" Lalitha replied, "No," and Dilip said, "Yes." Lalitha said it sounded like a whistle, like a horn, like a musical instrument, and Dilip said it sounded like someone was calling Soman. Eapen asked if the someone was a man or a woman. First Dilip said a man and then he said a woman and then he said he didn't know. So the day passed and then the next and the next until a week had passed. The police had been told by now, but they weren't taking this matter seriously. "Nobody runs away with a sound," they said, as did the neighbours, visiting relatives, and fishermen.

Aunts clucked their tongues and tried to smooth Lalitha's hair. They fed Dilip the sweet treats they had brought. But mostly the visitors stared and sighed. Lalitha grew annoyed by them, and within a week, she had had enough. She made everyone leave her house and decided she was going to drive Scootie by herself, so she could earn a little money for herself and Dilip. After all, they had to live, no? The next morning, Lalitha was ready as soon as the day broke. Her mother was going to get Dilip ready for school, while Lalitha left for the airport with Eapen so they could catch the passengers coming off the first flight from Delhi. Cochin marvelled to see a woman driving a scooter, but Cochin didn't like it. Other drivers whistled at Lalitha; some even made funny gestures and looked at her with sly smiles. Lalitha hated driving Scootie around. She hated the whistles, she hated being afraid, and she hated people staring. But what could she do? How was she to earn money if she didn't use Scootie? So she asked Eapen to keep checking up on her and to take the same routes that she got. Eapen tried, but it wasn't easy. "One person wants to go to the market, another one to the church. How to go to the same place, Lalitha?" said Eapen. But he tried.

One day, some months after Lalitha had started driving Scootie, a strange thing happened. Lalitha was at the airport with Eapen, waiting for the Delhi flight. As passengers strolled off the plane, she saw a man who gave her a jolt. He was a tall man, with a thin face and a beard. He almost looked like a foreigner, he was so fair, but he looked familiar. He looked around the scooties, ignoring all the drivers offering him bargain prices. Deliberately, he came to Lalitha, and said, "That's the scootie I want. How much for the day?" Lalitha had never been hired for the day before. She asked Eapen, "How much?" Eapen was considering what to say when the man from the Delhi flight said, "For the week." "For the week?" asked Lalitha in surprise. "Yes," answered the man. "I want to tour all over in a scootie for a week." "You take that one," said Lalitha, pointing to Eapen and Tony. The man refused. He wanted this scootie and this one only. He liked Scootie's wide-open back.

Lalitha named a price that would pay her enough money for the whole month. The man agreed and asked Lalitha to take him to a hostel. "Which hostel?" she asked, and he said he didn't care. Wherever she thought he could be comfortable and get good food. Lalitha couldn't think of any place like that except her mother's house. She said so and the man said, "Okay, let's go to your mother's house and she can feed me. I will pay two thousand rupees for the week." Lalitha was thrilled, but Eapen looked at her as if she was crazy. "Your mother's not even living in her house," he said. "She's living with you since Soman went away." "Oh," said Lalitha, remembering that her mother now lived with her. Well, the man could live there too, she thought. Why not? So she said, "It's okay, Eapen, not to worry. You come for dinner, hm? Bring some meen, no?" and with that she went off into Cochin with the man from Delhi.

When she brought the man home, her mother wasn't happy, even though she was glad about the money. "An unknown man," she said, "you never know what an unknown man can do." Lalitha answered drily, "You never know what a known man can do," and her mother quietly agreed to give the man the best room. The man from Delhi loved everything. He loved the lagoon at the back of the house. He loved the sea in the front. He loved the coconut trees all around. He didn't mind the cats. He didn't mind washing his hands and feet by the tap at the back of the house. He loved the breakfast of rice and peanuts. He wanted to sleep in the sun all morning, and then he wanted beer and fried fish for lunch. Lalitha and her mother were very happy. He's an easy man to please, they said to each other as they went about doing various tasks.

The first day, the man was very lazy. That night, after he'd eaten his dinner, he and Eapen sat under the trees in the moonlight. Lalitha was on the other side of the house, thinking of Soman. Dilip was asleep, and her mother was watching television. The sea whooshed just as it had on the night Soman disappeared. At the back of the house, Eapen was telling the man about Soman. The man listened intently, and then he brought out a flute from his bag. He played a note and then a second and a third. Lalitha heard the notes and her skin prickled. The sound was like the sound that had taken Soman away. She ran to the back of the house to see where the sound was coming from, but there was nothing there except the man from Delhi and Eapen.

The man was playing the flute. Irritably, she asked, "Where's that tooting coming from? Eapen, are you tooting?" Offended Eapen said, "Why would I toot?" The

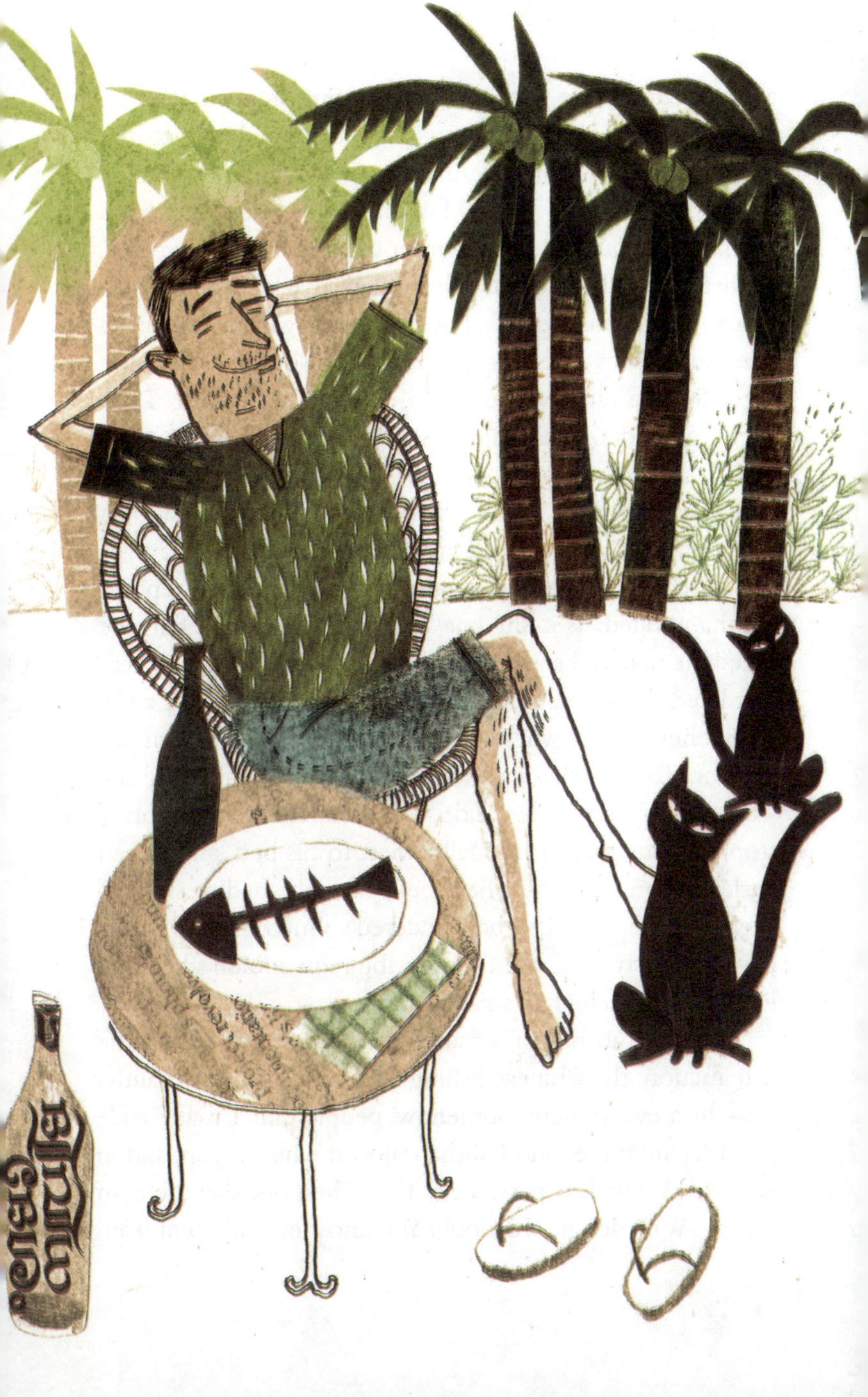

man put down the flute, and the tooting stopped at once. "You took my husband away," said Lalitha slowly to the man. He looked at her in surprise and said, "I don't know what you're talking about." Lalitha grabbed the flute from his hand and put it to her own mouth and blew. A horrible, distorted sound came out. She handed it back and said, "Play that sound again. Please." The man did. Again and again so that Lalitha was sure this was the sound she'd heard on the night Soman ran away. As if to confirm her feeling, Dilip came to the door, rubbing his sleepy eyes, saying, "Ma, Ma, there's the sound that took Pa away." Ma said yes it was and held him, but there was nothing to do. This man had just arrived from Delhi; he couldn't have taken Soman away.

Lalitha asked the man's name. "It's Namos," he replied. Lalitha nodded, as if she knew his name already. Then she asked the man to keep playing as she took Dilip back to bed. She liked the sound. She wondered if she could run away with it herself and where the sound might take her. But not tonight. Tonight she was not going outside again. No, she was going to stay safe inside with Dilip. Soon the tooting stopped. The man from Delhi went to his bed, and Eapen curled up on the sofa, where he insisted he had to sleep to keep everyone safe. Lalitha wondered about the man's name. It sounded strange, she thought, but she couldn't be sure. People from Delhi had strange names.

The next morning, the man from Delhi wanted to see the fish auction, the Chinese fishing nets, and a temple. Lalitha took him everywhere. Somehow, people didn't make rude remarks anymore, and Lalitha enjoyed whizzing around in Scootie. A few days passed like this. Then one day the man asked, "Who designed Scootie? You know he's different from all the other scooters." Lalitha looked proud and told the man that Soman had designed Scootie. "I would've designed Scootie the same way," said the man. "I would also give him a nice wide back." He added, "I wonder if we can do more with Scootie," as if to himself. Lalitha wondered what he meant. So she said, "What do you mean, 'do more,' and what do you mean, 'we'?" And the man answered that he wanted to live on Vypeen Island forever. Could he?

Lalitha opened her eyes wide. She said, "You can do anything. You're a rich man from Delhi." The man said that she hadn't understood, but it didn't matter. He wondered what could be done with Scootie. He went to Scootie and examined him closely. He touched his ruffled back gently, and Lalitha felt a little funny seeing him, but she didn't say anything. Then the man said he had an idea. He said he wanted to use Scootie as a "prototype" and Lalitha asked, "What's that?" The man said that he wanted Scootie to be the best example of a scootie because it was. He said, "I have to go away for a few days. May I take Scootie with me?" Lalitha said no. She said she needed Scootie for work to make money. The man offered to pay for Scootie, and he promised to bring him back in a month.

Lalitha did not like the idea of the man taking Scootie away but said she would think about it. The next morning she told the man he could not take Scootie with him. Namos looked puzzled when she told him that and asked her to rethink her decision. Lalitha said there was nothing to rethink. Scootie was her link to Soman, she said, and so she couldn't let him go. The man nodded like he understood and looked at her a long while. Then he said, "What if I leave you my flute while I am gone? That way, I will have Scootie, and you will have my flute." Lalitha was surprised by the man's offer, but it made her feel better saying yes to Namos. "Yes," she said, "this is a fair trade. You take Scootie and I will keep the toot." "The flute," Namos answered, but Lalitha had already wandered away.

Lalitha waved Scootie and Namos away the next day, holding his reed flute in her hand. After he'd left, she went inside and wandered from room to room. Dilip was in school, and her mother was preparing lunch in the kitchen. There was nothing for Lalitha to do without Scootie, so she went and sat at the back of the house and watched the cats prance around under the coconut trees. Then she put the flute to her mouth and blew into it. The sounds that emerged were awful. None of them sounded like any that Namos made or like the sound that took Soman away. Sadly, Lalitha went inside and put away the flute in a drawer in her bedroom.

That night, Lalitha, Dilip, and her mother had a quiet dinner. Afterwards, Lalitha brought out the flute because she was used to hearing it every night. She handed it to Dilip and said, "Why don't you try to play a sound?" Hesitantly, Dilip put the flute to his mouth. He blew softly, sure only angry sounds would come out. Instead, a low but pleasant sound emerged and hung in the air. Dilip blew into the flute again, this time more confidently, and soon soothing sounds could be heard, almost like the toots Dilip and his mother had heard many weeks ago with Soman.

So the days passed. Exactly a month after Namos had gone, he was back with a broad smile on his face and a very shiny Scootie in tow. He told Lalitha he was planning to open a new resort down the road. Would she come and see it? Lalitha said okay and took Dilip along. At the new hotel, small huts were mushrooming in front of the lagoon. And in the dining room, there was a bar and an open kitchen. But where there should have been tables, there were small scooties. All the tables looked like Scootie! Namos had tables put in front of the scooties' back seats, and he had made seats on the sides of the tables as well. Waiters could come and serve food through the scooties' wide-open backs. Did Lalitha like this, Namos asked? Lalitha thought this was a strange thing to do and said, "Why would anybody want to eat in a scootie?" But Dilip loved the scooties and was running from one to the other, wanting his lunch served from the back window. Lalitha saw how happy he was and then said she also liked the scooties. "Soman would be so proud to see a rich man from Delhi make tables from Scootie."

Namos asked Lalitha if she would work at the resort with Scootie. The man wanted her to be the official driver of the resort, and he wanted Scootie to be the official vehicle of the resort. The hotel would be called "Scooties on the Lagoon,"

because that's what it was. "Everyone loves scooties, especially people from Delhi," said the man. Lalitha looked puzzled, but she accepted the man's offer. "Okay," she said, "I'll come every day from my house to this resort and work here." "No," the man said, "we'll build a small house for you and your mother at the edge of the compound. It'll be better for Dilip, no?" Lalitha agreed again. Then the man said he was going to ask Eapen and Lalitha's mother to work for him also. "A new resort will need a lot of workers," he said. "So we'll all work for the resort, and in the evenings I'll play the flute. Doesn't that sound nice?" Lalitha said it did and Dilip nodded yes as well. Lalitha told Namos that Dilip now played the flute quite nicely. "What about you?" he asked, and Lalitha sadly shook her head no.

Eapen and Lalitha's mother were happy to be given new jobs. "Such a nice man," they said. "Look, the toot brought something back, hm? It took Soman away, but it brought the man from Delhi. He's from Delhi, no, even though he looks a foreigner?"

Everyone liked to hear the sound of Namos's flute in the evenings after dinner. Lalitha told Namos she understood why Soman would run away with such a nice sound. He said, "People have had to run away with different things. I ran away because of what I saw. See, now I don't live in Delhi because I saw Vypeen Island."

Lalitha nodded thoughtfully. Some nights, she felt, she herself might leave with the sound of Namos's flute.

Miss Hadd

Everyone called her Miss Hat, even though that was not her name. Her name was Miss Hadd. She lived by herself at the edge of the row of houses that lay at the edge of the small Texan town. Beyond the row of houses was a wide meadow on which the Indians lived in little shacks they had built with the wood and stones they found. Beyond where the Indians lived was the river. Everyone used the river. The white people picnicked by the river. The black people came there to have their babies baptised with a quick dunk into the flowing current just where the river curved. The Mexicans came across the border to the curve of the river as they had always done. The Indians came in the moonlight and lit a fire by the river. Pieces of flint and bits of the arrowheads they used could be found under the stones by the river years after all the Indians had left and moved into the big towns.

Miss Hadd had a large garden in which she grew green beans, potatoes, carrots, onions, garlic, and cosmos flowers. She loved the cosmos and made them ring around the garden so that white and pink flowers always waved to her on their thin stalks when she reached home. She worked as a cleaning woman at the college up the hill. Every morning at 5am, Miss Hadd left her house and walked up the hill to the college. All day long she bent and cleaned, first with a broom and then with a mop. Sometimes she even cleaned on her hands and knees, rubbing with a wet rag the dust that lay on the moulding near the floor. The floors of the college were a glistening pine. The moulding and the walls were a light white, clean and soothing in the Texan sun. Light slanted into the large rooms of the college and made the white whiter or yellower, depending on the time of the day. In the early evenings, when the light turned gold, Miss Hadd took a break from her cleaning. She did so in such a way that nobody noticed her standing on one side of the room, watching the bars of light slide in from the tall windows.

Her hands would move her mop mechanically, so if anybody saw her standing there, they would see a cleaning woman rubbing a stubborn stain off the floor.

Once the light was in her, Miss Hadd's workday was almost over. Then she would stack her pails and mops and brooms, and she would remove her white apron and cap and fold them up to take them home for a wash. Every day, Miss Hadd wore a fresh, starched apron and cap when she came to work. Before she went to bed at night, the cap and apron were washed and hung on the line above the cosmos in the garden. When Miss Hadd walked home with her bundle of clothes, she walked home filled with the tall yellow light of the college. When she reached her own quiet house with its low ceiling, its single long room with the narrow door in the front, she would allow the light to come out of her and fill her tiny kitchen as she prepared her dinner. The shotgun house on the edge of the row of houses on the edge of town would, for a short time, lose its dinginess.

On Sundays, Miss Hadd did not work, but she got up even earlier than on weekdays. After she was awake, she would step into her garden to see the first wisps of morning tinge the night. Her plants would sway and yield to her hand or to the breeze that drifted off the river. Miss Hadd talked to her plants on these mornings. She crooned to them and caressed them; she lifted them up and weighed their growth in her hands. If the okra was being stubborn, she would stroke it gently and urge it to let its yellow flower grow into the long, green, almost bristly vegetable she loved. The plants listened to her. Nobody had a garden as rich as Miss Hadd's. Even though everybody grew the same things, Miss Hadd always harvested more potatoes, more yams, and more carrots than anyone else. Everything she grew tasted sweeter as well. Some said she had magic in her fingers that had come all the way from Africa on the first boats that had crossed the Atlantic. Perhaps because her garden gave her so many vegetables, perhaps because they tasted so sweet, perhaps because she lived alone and people saw her go to the river before the first light on Sundays, they were scared of Miss Hadd. The adults never spoke to her. When they passed Miss Hadd, they nodded their heads and tipped their hats. "Mornin', Miss Hat," they said, and Miss Hadd never corrected them. "Morning," she would answer and walk on.

The children were frightened of Miss Hadd. They knew she lived alone. They had heard her talk to her plants. They had seen her muttering by the river, her hands in the water just where the river curved and babies were baptised. But when Miss Hadd invited the children to eat her sweet potatoes, the children could never refuse. Every year, Miss Hadd invited children to eat her potatoes. Shyly pushing each other forward, the children would forget their fear, and follow each other into the corner of the garden. Those who had tasted her potatoes—potatoes which easily split with a simultaneous push to their pointy ends so they opened like paper boats—could never forget their sweetness. It was like eating the low yellow sky of October.

First Miss Hadd made the children settle in the corner of the garden. The cosmos would wave around them, taller than the children huddled there. Then Miss Hadd would look for the tallest boy and the tallest girl. "You," she would point to the boy, and "You," she would point to the girl, and say, "Dig a hole for the fire," handing shovels to both. The boy and girl would step forward and start digging. Once they had dug a deep hole, Miss Hadd would have the other children carry forward the small twigs and branches she had gathered by the river. When the fire had been started in the moist earth, she made one or two children select fresh potatoes from those lying on a crooked shelf on the side of the garden. If there were ten children, then eleven sweet potatoes were picked. "You always need one extra for luck," she would say, and the children would agree as they took the sweet potatoes to the tap at the end of the garden to rinse the dry mud off them. Then with a heap of potatoes by the side of the hole where the fire burned, the children would gather close to each other. Soon, they knew, Miss Hadd would tell her stories. She would tell stories until the potatoes were soft enough to be sucked into the children's mouths, the moist and buttery inside followed by the scorched crispness outside.

The children were scared of Miss Hadd. But by now they were peering into the fire to see if all the sticks had burned and made coal for the potatoes. Miss Hadd squatted by the fire, while the children sat full on their behinds. Miss Hadd never fidgeted; she never moved, as if she had sat on her haunches all her life. Occasionally, Miss Hadd stirred the fire and let the fresh coals tumble on each other with a long stick she held in her hand. The children tried to sit quietly, trying not to push each other to see how red the coals were in the pit. Once the coals were ready, once a fresh greyness covered their red, Miss Hadd dropped the sweet potatoes into their glow. Then she covered the coals with the newly dug earth lying on the side of the hole. Only then would she start her stories. The children were scared of Miss Hadd's stories just as they were scared of her. She made people sick who were not. For her, delicate flowers grew tall and strong like trees.

Perhaps it was because her stories were true that the children were scared of Miss Hadd. But by now the potatoes were in the fire, and the children knew that no potato they ate would taste as sweet or yield as softly as the one cooking in that earth.

Miss Hadd's low voice would ask, "What do you want in your story?" and each child would name one thing. "A pig," "a woman," "a cat," "the storm," "a boat," "a river," "Christmas," and the list would go on until each child had made their choice. Miss Hadd would listen carefully, the long stick she had used to stir the fire scratching the thing each child wanted into the soft earth. Then she would stare at the list in the mud and start her story. "Once upon a time a cat went to the river…," she would begin and the children would huddle closer as the story Miss Hadd told meandered over the many things written in the mud. From time to time, as a strange animal no one had heard of jumped across the wide plains in another world, he brought with him the whiff of sweet potatoes roasting in a closed pit in the earth. The children would fidget at the smell. Sometimes the little ones would start crying as they listened to their familiar pig, cat or woman become strange and frightening in Miss Hadd's story. The pig might have grown horns before he flew away, or the cat might have helped an old woman speak to the dead by a dry river. The woman might have lived in a village where it never rained, so she had to ask for a storm by praying to the gods of the sky and the earth and the dead. Miss Hadd would look into the wide frightened eyes of the children, but her low voice wouldn't pause. None of the children dared to speak.

Once Miss Hadd saw a boy looking doubtful as she spoke of the storm the woman had called. Miss Hadd got angry and, hitting her stick against the pit where the potatoes roasted, she said, "You don't believe me. All my stories are true, even though you tell me what you want in the story. All my stories are true." Then she looked into the clear Texan sky where the light was disappearing in large swathes of red and orange and yellow. "You don't believe a woman can call for a storm? Well, I will call for a storm tonight. By the time you have eaten your potatoes, you'll see rain fall on you." Miss Hadd looked so angry that nobody dared whisper that the clear Texan night could not cloud over with a storm tonight. Instead, the children huddled closer together and thought of the potatoes that would soon be ready.

By the time Miss Hadd's story ended, unknown beasts had jumped across more plains because the storm that the woman had called didn't stop. It rained for days and days, and the earth became so wet that everywhere was a river. The village people asked the woman to leave and seek help to dry out the skies. She steered her boat along the river, but she did not go forward. Instead, the river flowed down through a chasm into the earth and the woman went

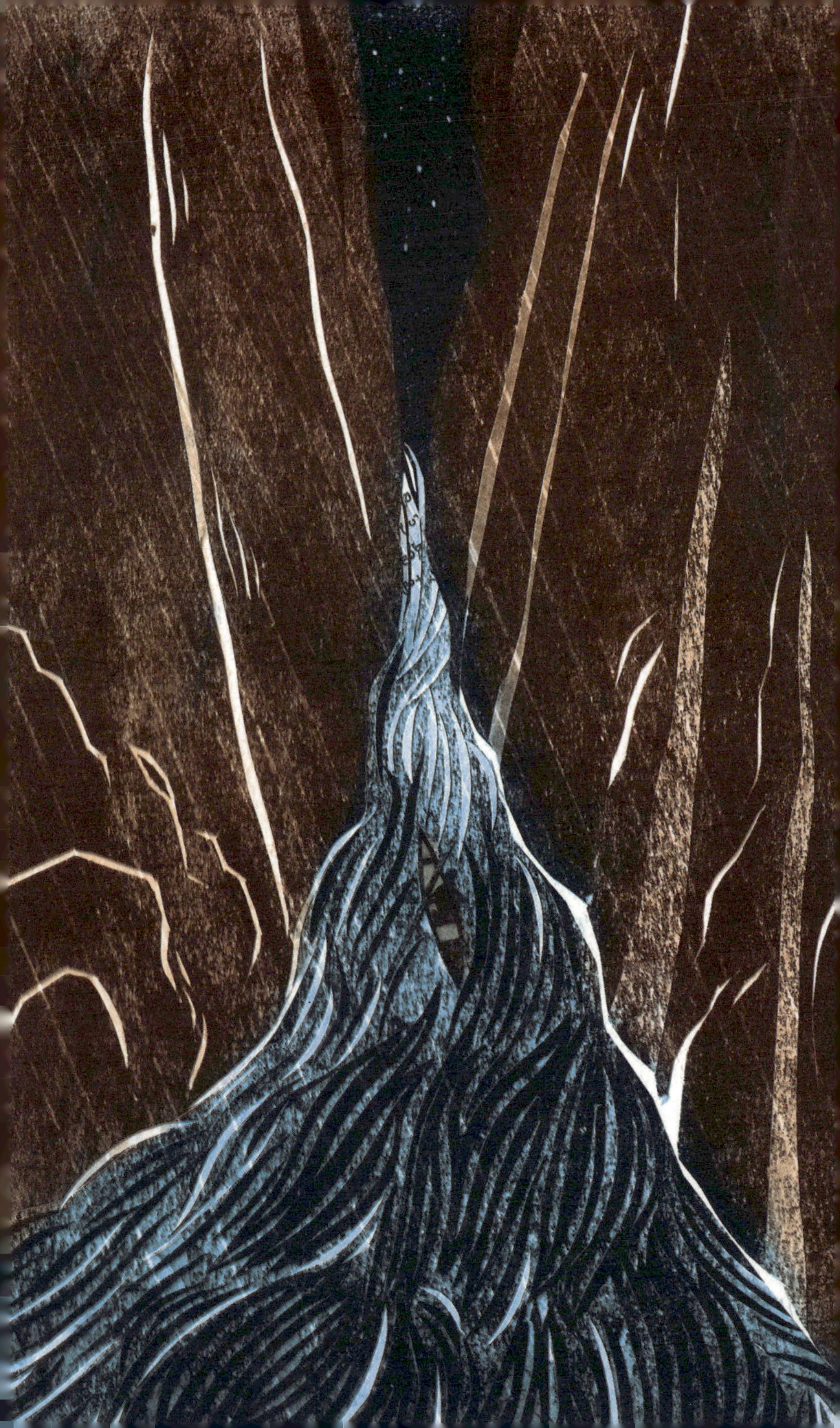

deeper and deeper into the dark. There she found a person who could help, but to make the storm stop the woman had to agree never to return. Centuries later she could still be found steering her boat along a river that flowed back into the earth, where cries for help were never heard. By this time, the children were holding each other in fear. Some wanted to run, but they couldn't move, and then Miss Hadd stopped speaking and started breaking away the earth which covered the pit of potatoes. She scooped the potatoes out with a shovel and asked a child to take a clean rag and dust off the grey ash that covered them. She laid the potatoes out on a flat tray and let them cool for a few moments before squeezing each one by pressing its ends together. In the steaming basins they made, she dropped generous dollops of white, homemade butter. Miss Hadd placed a warm potato in each eager outstretched hand and watched greedy mouths attach immediately to them to suck out their orange flesh.

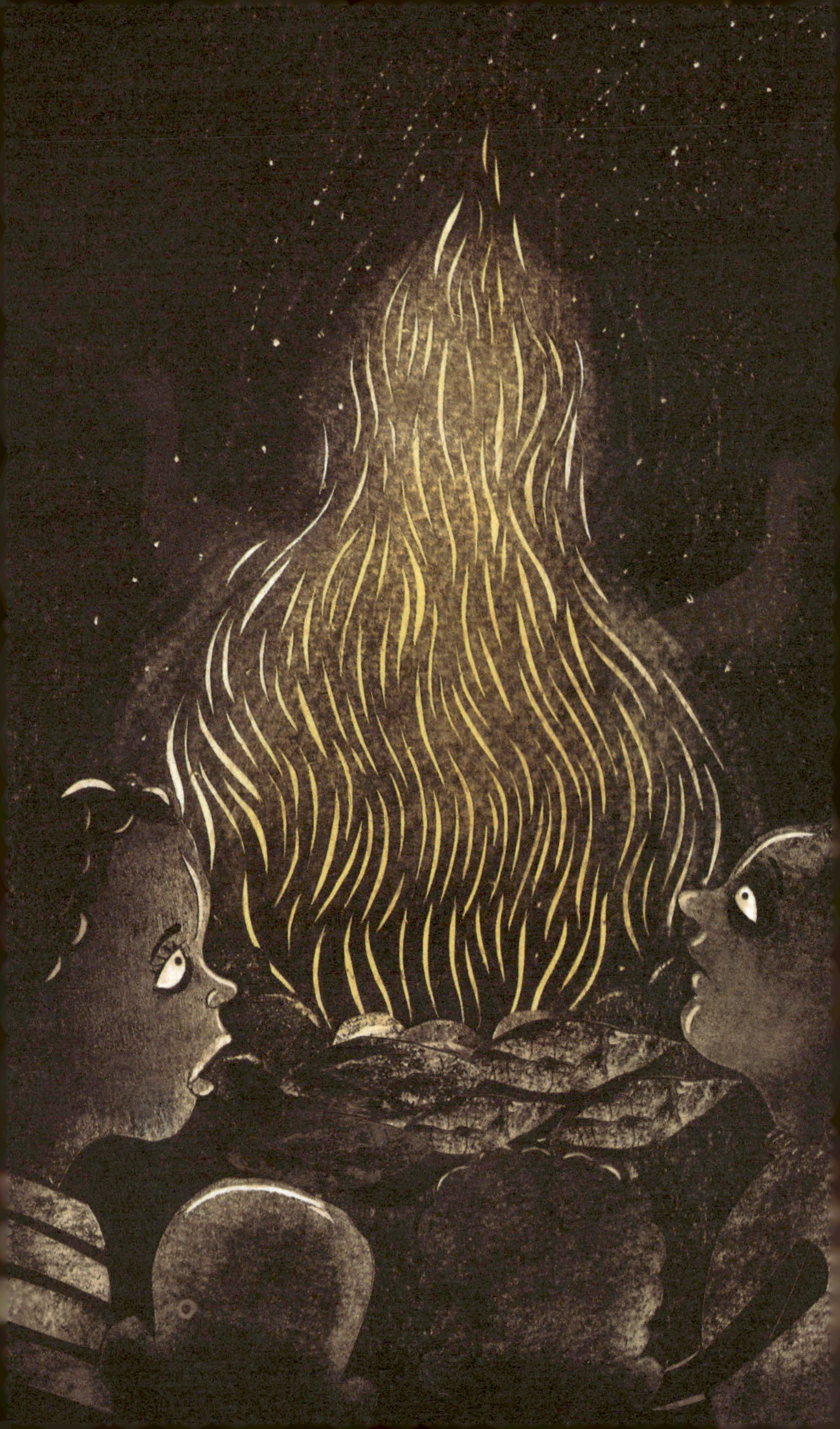

Miss Hadd ate two potatoes, the one that had been counted for her and the extra one for luck. As the children tucked the crumpled, crisp skin of their potatoes into their mouths, Miss Hadd smiled at them, but they didn't smile back. Soon the children started fidgeting and along with Miss Hadd looked up into the sky to follow a streak of lightning slide all the way down into the garden. The children covered their ears against the coming thunder as Miss Hadd said, "I told you my stories are true." She rose off her haunches to watch children scatter to their homes in the sudden rain. Inside their houses, children clung to their mothers and stayed close to the wood fire even though it wasn't cold. Miss Hadd stayed out in the rain, looking at the cosmos fall around her.

About the Author

Padmini Mongia teaches literature in English at Franklin and Marshall College. She is a teacher and scholar, a writer and painter. *Pchak, Pchak: A Story of Crocodiles* appeared in 2008 and a solo show, *Reach*, concluded in December 2016.